AF077360

For Aileen, lover of onions and murder.
Claire

This book is dedicated to my many enemies.
Alasdair

This is a work of fiction. Names, characters, places and incidents are either the product of the author's imagination or, if real, used fictitiously. All statements, activities, stunts, descriptions, information and material of any other kind contained herein are included for entertainment purposes only and should not be relied on for accuracy or replicated as they may result in injury.

First published 2023 by
Walker Books Ltd
87 Vauxhall Walk, London SE11 5HJ

2 4 6 8 10 9 7 5 3 1

Text © 2023 Alasdair Beckett-King
Illustrations © 2023 Claire Powell

The right of Alasdair Beckett-King and Claire Powell to be identified as author and illustrator respectively of this work has been asserted in accordance with the Copyright, Designs and Patents Act 1988

This book has been typeset in EB Garamond, Caveat, ITC American Typewriter, Fjalla One, Dina's Handwriting, Uncle Edward, Burbank and Blogger Sans.

Printed and bound by CPI Group (UK) Ltd, Croydon CR0 4YY

All rights reserved. No part of this book may be reproduced, transmitted or stored in an information retrieval system in any form or by any means, graphic, electronic or mechanical, including photocopying, taping and recording, without prior written permission from the publisher.

British Library Cataloguing in Publication Data:
a catalogue record for this book is available from the British Library

ISBN 978-1-5295-0581-8

www.walker.co.uk

MONTGOMERY BONBON

DEATH AT THE LIGHTHOUSE

ALASDAIR BECKETT-KING
ILLUSTRATED BY **CLAIRE POWELL**

Chapter One
Odde Island

The most troublesome thing about being a detective is that it is almost impossible to go on holiday.

That was what Bonnie was thinking to herself, seated in the old grey ice-cream van as it rumbled across the causeway to Odde Island. The vehicle's name was Bessie, and Grampa Banks was in the driver's seat. The former ice-cream vendor was snappily dressed as always, with a tailored cardigan and a silk cravat. His old-fashioned camera swung around his neck on a strap, bouncing every time Bessie hit a pothole.

Next to Grampa Banks was his granddaughter, Bonnie Montgomery.

Let us be clear: Bonnie was not a detective. She was an ordinary girl from a town called Widdlington – one of the most ordinary places in the entire galaxy. Ordinary ten-year-olds are not, ordinarily, allowed to go around solving mysteries. Everybody knows that. But, by an extraordinary coincidence, the world's finest detective had a tendency to show up wherever Bonnie went.

Montgomery Bonbon was not a tall man. In fact, he was exactly the same height as Bonnie. He was never seen without his signature beret and his battered old raincoat. A distinguished black moustache bristled proudly underneath his nose, and when he spoke, it was with *the foreign accent most mystérieux, non?*

No one knew that Bonnie Montgomery and the celebrated

BONBON FLUSHES OUT POOPER!

foreign sleuth were one and the same person. No one apart from Bonbon's loyal assistant and Bonnie's loving grandfather, Grampa Banks. This was why Bonnie never got to enjoy a holiday. She rarely had time to unpack her bucket and spade before she found herself slapping on her alter ego's fabulous false moustache.

"I've always wanted to visit Odde Island," said Grampa Banks, as much to himself as to Bonnie. "The lighthouse, the beaches and the pageant – it's meant to be a right royal spectacle."

Grampa Banks's enthusiasm was starting to rub off on Bonnie. This little getaway *had* to go more smoothly than their recent stay at Pinshaw Waterslide Park. That holiday had been ruined when Montgomery Bonbon had been called upon to track down the infamous Pinshaw Pooper. (Tragically, Bonnie and Grampa Banks were too late to stop the park's number one log flume becoming a number *two* log flume.) And their last camping trip had been all but ruined when the great detective found himself on the trail of the Green Phantom of Crumberley End. The creature, which had so terrorized campers, turned out to be Grampa Banks wearing his nightly avocado face mask.

With Bonbon around, even something as pleasant as a visit to a museum was liable to end in cold-blooded murder. Detectives are drawn towards mystery, you see – like new wellington boots towards a great big muddy puddle.

Bonnie looked out of the passenger window and saw the North Sea stretching away towards the horizon. Driving on Odde Causeway made her feel like a stone skimming across the surface of the water. It was a very strange kind of road, because it was only a road when the tide was out. In a few hours, the autumn sun would set, the tide would come in and Odde Causeway would

disappear beneath the waves. The island that was rising up before them would be completely cut off from the rest of the world, until the tide went out again.

Ahead, the sandy road gave way to pebbly beaches and treeless cliffs topped with long shaggy grass waving in the wind. To Bonnie, the craggy rocks looked like funny faces wearing glorious green wigs. The lopsided island sloped up, up, up towards its famous lighthouse. Bonnie felt lucky. The storms of the previous night had cleared up, just in time for their arrival, and now the sun shone down on the island, bathing it in a rosy gold light.

"There it is," said Grampa Banks, nudging Bonnie cheerfully. "Odde Island!"

He was an experienced detective's assistant, so he rarely missed little details like that.

"And if you think that's good, just wait for the pageant. They've got fireworks and face painting and fabulous costumes. There's a parade across the island, like summat you've never seen before. Sounds grand, doesn't it? A week without murder." He glanced at Bonnie, radiating optimism. "Just the ticket, eh?"

Bonnie smiled back at Grampa Banks. A week without murder did indeed sound grand. From the moment she had kissed her mum goodbye, Bonnie had been looking forward to watching the Odde Island Pageant, visiting the island's famous clockwork lighthouse, digging a great big hole on the beach and then getting a bit bored.

She had stuffed Montgomery Bonbon's disguise into her favourite yellow backpack and hidden it in her bedroom at home in Widdlington. Now Bonnie was free to have a quiet little holiday without mystery or intrigue or shenanigans of any kind. And nothing was going to stop her.

CLANG!

A red and white striped barrier crashed down across the road ahead, like an executioner's axe. Grampa Banks's reflexes had been honed over many years of driving Bessie. You never knew when an ice-cream enthusiast was going to leap out in front of you, in search of a Raspberry Surprise. A crêpe-soled shoe slammed into the brake.

SCREEEEEEE!

Bonnie felt herself lurch forward as the van squealed to a halt. Her hand flew to her face to stop her moustache from whizzing off and sticking to the windscreen. At the last second, she remembered that she was not wearing it.

"Flamin' Nora!" cried Grampa Banks, before adding, "Pardon my language" under his breath.

Grampa Banks was an excellent driver, and he was not a man who easily lost his cool. But Bonnie knew there was one thing he could not stand, and that was *rudeness.* Clattering a barrier down in front of two innocent holidaymakers seemed exceedingly rude to Bonnie. Her grandfather's eyebrows had little experience when it came to frowning, but they were making a good go of it now.

"What the bloomin' heck is this all about?" he asked no one in particular.

The striped barrier was attached to a small building, raised up from the beach on funny wooden stilts. According to a weather-beaten sign, it was the Odde Island Excise House. A little door opened, and Bonnie saw a man emerge. He carried a clipboard and there was a brass bugle dangling from his belt. The man was completely bald, apart from a tiny quiff on the top of his head fluttering in the sea breeze. He marched down a flight of steps towards Bessie, wedged a tiny pair of glasses onto the end of his nose and rapped smartly on the driver's window.

As Grampa Banks wound down the window, the man lifted the brass bugle to his lips and blew a short, sharp, eardrum-shattering... **PARP!**

"Oi!" said Grampa Banks, jamming his fingers in his ears. "What d'you think you're playing at?!"

Instead of answering, the man took a deep, deep breath. It was so deep Bonnie was convinced she could see tufts of grass bending towards him. Then he began to read from his clipboard.

"ON behalf of the Odde Island ORDER of the Golden Fleece, it is MY privilege to welcome you in YOUR capacity as most welcome visitors TO our island..."

Back in Widdlington, the inhabitants of Odde Island were known as Oddities, and Bonnie was beginning to see why. She glanced between the strange man and Grampa Banks, who was now frowning so hard his eyebrows had formed one big angry monobrow.

"Now, look here—" began Grampa Banks, but the Oddity continued.

"...and IN my capacity as Iain Percival, exciseman-in-chief OF Odde Island, permit me to remind you that ALL varieties of the bulb *Allium cepa* ARE held as contraband herein, heretofore, hereupon and hereafter."

Grampa Banks looked at Bonnie, obviously hoping she had made sense of all that waffle. She shook her head.

"Excuse me?" said Grampa Banks.

"On Odde Island," said Iain Percival impatiently, as if this were the most obvious thing in the world, "onions are banned!"

"You what?" spluttered Grampa Banks.

"By order of the Order of the Golden Fleece," added Iain Percival, as if that explained anything.

The exciseman thrust a pamphlet into Grampa Banks's hands. It was entitled *Know Your Onions* and it had a picture of an onion on the front with a big cross through it.

"Well," puffed Grampa Banks, tucking the

pamphlet into his cardigan and coaxing his eyebrows back into their usual positions, "we haven't got any onions. Not a single one. So you can open up your little barrier and we'll be on our merry—"

Bonnie coughed, and both men turned to look at her.

"We ... um..." she began. "We haven't quite finished this bag of Cheese and Onion Crunchy Puffs..."

She crinkled a half-empty crisp packet out from one of Bessie's crevices, and Iain Percival reacted as if she had slapped him in the face with wet seaweed.

"Contrabaaaaand!" he exclaimed. "Call the Onion Disposal Unit!"

The Onion Disposal Unit turned out to be Iain Percival wearing a large hat that said *Onion Disposal Unit* and wielding a large wooden mallet. He glared at Bonnie and Grampa Banks while he smashed the offending Crunchy Puffs flat with the mallet.

"Flagrant disregard for local ordinances!"

CRUNCH!

"Endangering the delicate noses of islanders AND the sensitive beaks of indigenous seabirds!"

CRUNCH!

"I could turn you both away right now!"

CRUNCH!

Bonnie had never seen such a big fuss over nothing. And she had once witnessed Inspector Prashanti Sands, Widdlington Constabulary's most plodding detective, attempting to run the Splat the Rat stall at the town fête. By the end of the day, the inspector had arrested three children, kicked a vicar and splatted a bottle of fizzy wine.

Eventually, after scribbling copious notes on his clipboard, Iain Percival let Grampa Banks off with a stern warning. The barrier finally lifted, Bessie grumbled back into life and rolled on.

Bonnie Montgomery was on holiday ... at last.

"That business about the Order of the Golden Fleece," began Grampa Banks, "did that make any sense to you?"

"Nope!" said Bonnie, watching the road rise up and down as undulating sand dunes turned into grassy hillocks. They were heading for Odde Harbour, the multicoloured scattering of buildings that was the closest thing to a town on the island.

"It didn't strike you as ... *mysterious* at all?" he asked.

"Well," admitted Bonnie, "it was a bit weird, I suppose. But this is *Odde* Island."

"You can say that again. That Percival bloke is more waffly than a Belgian buffet. But look at me, worrying about nothing. The important thing is, we are going to have a lovely time, right?"

"Right," said Bonnie with determination.

"And nobody," said Grampa Banks, "and I mean *nobody*, is going to get murdered. Right?"

"Right!"

Wrong.

Chapter Two

The "Accident"

It might have been a funny place, but Odde Island was certainly beautiful, with its round hills and crooked crags and meandering drystone walls. At every bend in the winding road, Bonnie saw little signs planted in the ground. One said:

Another over there said:

And Bonnie could have sworn she saw one that just said:

> DON'T.

The sun was shining warmly now, but a cloud still seemed to hang over the islanders. On the approach to Odde Harbour, Bonnie saw folk replacing slates that had been blown off their roofs the night before, like playing cards swept off the table by a bad loser. She saw one local grimacing as he pulled armfuls of soggy bunting out of a hedgerow. Root vegetables and gourds with funny faces painted on them had been scattered hither and thither, and a woman in a large flowery hat was collecting them up and popping them into a wicker basket.

Bonnie could not help noticing that there was not an onion among them. Iain Percival would have approved.

The storm had clearly put something of a dampener on the preparations for the pageant, but Bonnie was not going to let that spoil her holiday.

"Well now," said Grampa Banks, speaking in the slow, deliberate voice he used when he was driving, "what do you reckon we should do first, love?"

"Check into the B & B & B & B?" asked Bonnie.

They were booked into the Bright Phoebus Bed & Breakfast. Bonnie had pointed out that, since they were staying for several nights, that made it a bed and breakfast and bed and breakfast and bed and breakfast and bed and breakfast...

"I mean, what are we going to do *after* we check into the B & B & B & B and ... oh, blimey!" muttered Grampa Banks, adjusting his new driving glasses.

"What's the matter?"

"Oh dear, dear, dear," he said, bringing Bessie to a stop next to a carefully tended little green.

Grampa Banks stepped out onto Odde Harbour, and Bonnie clambered down after him. The smell of salt and underwater things stung her nostrils. She heard the fizzle of the sea foam, and the gentle *clonk-clonk* of little boats at their moorings. The streets were cobbled, and the colourful buildings had an unsettling tendency to be wider at the top than they

were at the bottom. If Odde Harbour was a picture-book town, then the artist responsible had a thing or two to learn about architecture.

Bonnie followed her grandfather onto the green, where an aged display board showed an exquisitely detailed map of Odde Island. A *You are here* arrow pointed towards the harbour, and a woman dressed a bit like a police officer was pasting a large hand-lettered notice onto the other side of the map:

Oh no. Grampa Banks had been enthusing about Leerie Lighthouse for weeks. It was the last clockwork lighthouse in the world, as he had reminded her three times already that morning. It was also one of Odde Island's hottest attractions among cardigan-wearing older gentlemen. And it was closed.

"Pardon me ... erm ... Officer?" said Grampa Banks hesitantly. "Are you part of this Order of the Golden...?"

The woman pasting the notice wore a black helmet and when she smiled, the chinstrap squeezed her face into a perfect circle.

"Fleece? Ha! Hardly," she said, giving a clumsy salute. "Especial Constable Roz Baillie, at your service."

Bonnie was not quite sure what to make of that. Roz looked like she had cobbled her uniform together out of things you might find in the cupboard under the stairs. The plume on top of her helmet was definitely the head of a mop.

"What's a special constable?" Bonnie asked.

"Hello there, young lady – what an intelligent question," said Roz, folding her hands behind her back and adopting the warm but patronizing tone Bonnie was used to hearing when she was not dressed as Montgomery Bonbon. "I'm an *especial* constable. It's my job to keep the peace for the Order of the Golden Fleece in the run-up to the pageant. I'm not actually a real copper. More like a volunteer."

She thought for a moment. "Except they don't give you a choice about doing it. Pretty much everything that happens on Odde Island happens with the Order's say-so."

"But what actually *is* the Order?" asked Bonnie. "We don't have an order of the golden *anything* back in Widdlington."

"Oh, you know..." Roz paused for longer this time. "It's like a cross between a parish council and the Spanish Inquisition. They make all the rules, organize the pageant, boss folk around. It's tradition! The members are elected by the residents of Odde Island. Although ... the same people end up being voted in every year. That's tradition too."

"And has the Order really closed the lighthouse?" Bonnie asked, hoping perhaps that the notice was a decoy and tenacious tourists would still be allowed to visit. "My grampa was super keen to see it."

"I was super keen to see it," Grampa Banks agreed sadly. "It's the last clockwork lighthouse in the world, you know."

"We know," said Bonnie and Roz simultaneously.

"I'm very sorry but it's completely closed to the public," continued the especial constable. "I'm sure you understand why ... under the circumstances."

Bonnie and Grampa Banks blinked at her blankly.

"Oh my goodness," cried Roz, putting her hand over her mouth. "You haven't heard about the accident, have you?"

Bonnie and Grampa Banks exchanged a look. The words *the accident* rarely referred to anything good. It was never a marshmallow explosion, or someone ordering too many puppies.

A shudder seemed to pass through Roz Baillie. She placed a hand on Grampa Banks's elbow, led him a few wordless paces to the edge of the green, and pointed. In the distance, Bonnie could make out Leerie Lighthouse looming over the island.

Bonnie took a step closer, ever so quietly, to hear what Roz had to say.

"Last night, during the storm ... the lantern at the top of the lighthouse stopped turning."

"Stopped turning?" repeated Grampa Banks.

Roz nodded. "When folks went to investigate, they found the lighthouse keeper, Maude Cragge. Or rather, they found her body. The winds had blown her off the top of the lighthouse and she had fallen to her death. Horrible! The poor thing was taken away this morning. With Maude being the Grand Maven of the Order ... well ... we're all just trying our best to keep going."

Oh no, thought Bonnie.

"I'm sorry for your loss, Constable Baillie," said Grampa Banks softly.

Something in Roz's reaction told Bonnie that the especial constable was not deeply in mourning for the late Maude Cragge.

"Well, it's a dreadful thing to say," Roz whispered, "but I don't think Maude will be missed by many people around here. Loved having everything done *her way*, did our Maude. Still, an accident is an accident."

Bonnie had to bite the bullet. She had to know. She cleared her throat and Roz swung round to face her.

"And it was ... *definitely* an accident?" Bonnie asked.

Roz nodded. "Oh, a tragic accident! Absolutely tragic."

Bonnie breathed a small sigh of relief and took Grampa Banks's hand. "Perhaps it's time we—"

"Although," added Roz, "there was something a little bit ... *off* about the lighthouse this morning."

"Off?" Bonnie felt her upper lip twitch. "What kind of *off*?"

"I couldn't quite put my finger on it, but something about the scene just didn't make sense…"

Bonnie had questions. So many questions! But before she could assemble her thoughts, Roz shook her head, mop-top wobbling ludicrously.

"Oh, I'm just being silly! You folks enjoy your stay on the island."

Roz gathered up a stack of notices and a bucket of paste, and left Bonnie and Grampa Banks on the green. Bonnie's heart was sinking, because she knew that the especial constable was not being silly. She was being a detective.

A good detective is always on the lookout for things that are *off*, out of place, askew or unexplained. When Montgomery Bonbon caught the Coney Gang selling counterfeit rabbits, it all came down to Bonnie spotting a single hare out of place. On another occasion, the disappearance of Widdlington's lord mayor was explained when Montgomery Bonbon noticed that the mayor's massive gold necklace had been stolen and replaced with a note that read: *So long, suckers!*

And, of course, the perplexing theft of Grampa Banks's driving glasses was solved when Bonnie reminded him that they were on the top of his head. This happened almost every day.

Bonnie might have been left with questions. Who were the members of this Order of the Golden Fleece? What, for that matter, was a grand maven? But in her gut, she knew one thing: Roz Baillie had spotted a *clue* in Leerie Lighthouse. And where there were clues, there were crimes. She could see that Grampa Banks knew it too. He was already on his way back to Bessie with an air of resignation.

He unlocked the ice-cream van's rear door.

"Looks like there's summat up at the lighthouse, eh, love?"

He clambered inside and rummaged around in a long-defunct chest freezer, scattering old choc-ice wrappers everywhere. Bonnie craned her neck to see what he was doing.

"I suppose it's a good thing, then, that I decided to bring ... this."

Grampa Banks pulled a yellow backpack out of

the freezer. He must have discovered its hiding place and finagled it on board under Bonnie's nose. That backpack contained one beret, one raincoat and one moustache. As soon as she saw it, Bonnie knew her holiday was over.

Montgomery Bonbon's investigation had begun.

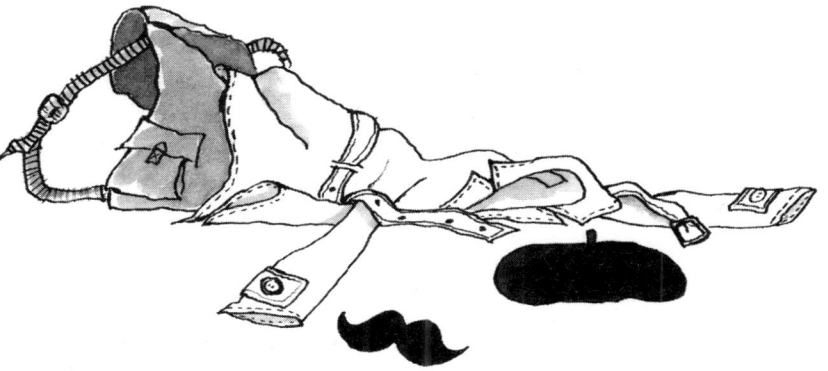

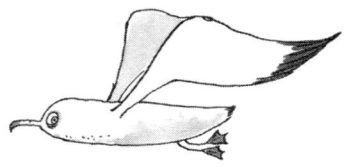

Chapter Three
The Golden Fleece

There was something fishy about Odde Island. And it was not just the general smell of the place.

Bonnie and Grampa Banks left the cobbles of Odde Harbour almost as quickly as they had arrived. The B & B & B & B was forgotten, for now, and Bessie began zipping across the island towards Leerie Lighthouse. But, as the road grew steeper and steeper, the zipping turned into grumbling. Before long, the grumbling became trundling. Grampa Banks soon had no choice but to stop at the bottom of the rocky outcrop named Solan Cliffs.

Here and there, strange white circles had been chalked onto the rock face. The work of local teens, no doubt. If you believed the newspapers, local teens were responsible for just about everything.

Bonnie squidged her moustache into position and gave it a few test wiggles in the rear-view mirror. It was firmly in place. She could not deny that it felt good to be Montgomery Bonbon at a moment like this: the start of a mystery.

She stepped out of the van and looked up at the site of Maude Cragge's demise. Leerie Lighthouse stood so lofty and tall that Bonnie reckoned it had to be visible from almost everywhere on the island. In her imagination, the seagulls wheeling and circling above could have been vultures. The lantern at the top was turning. It shone its bright beam all around as the setting sun turned the sky from gold to purple.

The lighthouse was painted in white, with a happy red stripe swooping round the middle. But white, Bonnie knew, was the colour of lies – and red was the colour of danger.

A network of narrow, uneven stairs had been cut slickly into the dark rock, as if with the world's biggest butter knife. It would have been impossible to ride a bike up towards the lighthouse, and unthinkable to get any closer in Bessie. Grampa Banks eyed the glassy-smooth steps with trepidation.

"You don't suppose they have an escalator, do you?" he asked grimly.

Bonnie hopped up the first step and turned towards her grandfather.

"The game is afoot, *mein ami*," she announced.

"Fair enough," he sighed, "but it always seems to be *our* feet doing the work."

Bonnie bounded up towards the lighthouse, while Grampa Banks steadily puffed his way up behind her. As she climbed higher, the crash of the waves below grew louder. How high had the water come on the night of the storm? Bonnie wondered. How fierce were the winds? Even now, with the storm over and the wind relatively gentle, the tapering tower seemed to hum as it sliced the breeze in two.

As Bonnie reached the little plateau on which the lighthouse stood, she could feel her detective's brain warming up underneath Bonbon's beret. She began to pace slowly around the lighthouse with her hands clasped behind her back. The ruffled grass at the foot of the tower showed no signs of the spot where the lighthouse keeper had landed. Wind and rain had swept away any details which might have helped Bonnie make sense of what had happened to poor Maude Cragge the night before.

She turned her attention to the top of the lighthouse. She could see a railing that protected the viewing deck around the lantern itself. A stiff gust of wind tousled her hair, inflated her raincoat and threatened to blow her beret out to sea. But it would have taken a very, very strong wind to carry a whole person over the railing. There was no sign of broken metal or even rust.

"Most strange," murmured Bonnie to herself in Montgomery Bonbon's voice.

She completed two full circles of the lighthouse before Grampa Banks heaved himself up the final few steps. While he was still mopping his brow, Bonnie went up to the lighthouse's whitewashed wooden door and reached for the handle.

"Hold up there, Bonbon old fruit!" called Grampa Banks. "The especial constable did say this place was off-limits."

Grampa Banks could not *really* have expected Bonnie to come all this way and leave the lighthouse un-snooped. She knew exactly what her grandfather had in mind as she sidled over to him and out of the corner of her mouth muttered, "Put it on the Tab?"

The Tab was an exhaustive catalogue of every rule Bonnie broke, every guideline she bent, and every NO ENTRY sign she limboed under while solving crimes as Montgomery Bonbon. Grampa Banks was already pulling out the familiar notebook from his back pocket. He flipped through page after page of transgressions.

THE TAB (CONT'D)

- DEFLATING A BOUNCY CASTLE
- DEFOLIATING A FLORIST
- DEFENESTRATING A BEEFEATER

Grampa Banks found a gap and with a little yellow pencil added:

- DEFYING OFFICIAL SIGNAGE

He snapped the notebook closed, and calmly informed Bonnie that she would be doing the washing-up until she was thirty-seven.

"*Merci*," said Bonnie. "Now let us begin."

The lighthouse door had one of the especial constable's notices pasted on it.

But that did not stop it swinging open at Bonnie's touch.

She had never seen the inside of a lighthouse before, never mind the last working clockwork lighthouse in the world. Oily chains, jaggy-toothed gears and pitch-black counterweights whirred and ticked and whizzed and tocked with exquisite precision.

At the bottom of the tower, in the centre of the room, was a large crank handle – for winding up the mechanism, Bonnie deduced. The electric lights were stained yellow and seemed to flicker as waves crashed against the rocks below, giving the impression that the strange mechanism was illuminated by candlelight.

Bonnie felt like she had been shrunk down and dropped inside an elderly gentleman's pocket watch. A spiral staircase curved its way around the outer wall, its ornate balustrade gleaming. A green telephone mounted on the wall looked like it could have had pride of place in an antiques shop. Maude Cragge had obviously run a tight ship. Or lighthouse.

And there was something else, glimmering on the opposite side of the circular room. A jacket the colour of polished gold hung on a coat hook.

"*Regardez*, the golden fleece!"

Of course. It made sense that the Grand Maven of the Order of the Golden Fleece would actually *have* a golden fleece of her own.

Click, FLASH, grrr...

Grampa Banks captured a snapshot of the golden fleece with his old-fashioned film camera.

"It looks more like a sort of golden *parka* to me,"

he said, squinting through the viewfinder. "The hood's all fuzzy."

Grampa Banks was right about the hood, which had a shock of golden fur like a lion's mane. It certainly appeared to be a fine piece of work. Bonnie reached out and touched a sleeve: lightweight, waterproof and luxuriously warm. Her fingers wriggled nimbly into the jacket's pockets and closed around a piece of paper. A clue? A poison pen letter? A treasure map? She pulled it out.

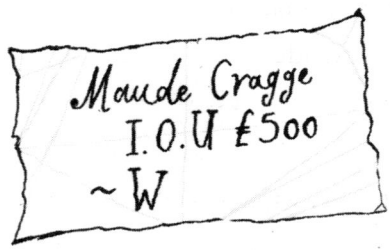

"Found something?" enquired Grampa Banks.

"It is an IOU for five hundred pounds," said Bonnie. "But who is W?"

Bonnie snaffled the IOU away in her raincoat and turned her attention to the wall around the fleece. It was decorated with plans for this year's Odde Island

Pageant. There were drawings of funny-looking floats and fish-faced costume designs initialled MC.

On a nearby workbench, Bonnie noticed framed photographs from previous pageants. One picture showed a parade of locals snaking across the island in even more outlandish outfits. Another showed the members of the Order standing at the top of a small hill.

She clocked Iain Percival immediately. Bonnie was not going to forget the man who had bugled Grampa Banks in a hurry. She recognized Miss Bunch as the flowery woman she had seen tending to street decorations in Odde Harbour. Then there were Tobias Waterman, Lady Wallop and Maanvi Mallick. The woman wearing the golden fleece was the late lighthouse keeper Maude Cragge.

Perhaps it was the influence of the clockwork lighthouse, but the cogs in Bonnie's brain began to turn a little faster.

"Tell to me if this is correct," Bonnie said to Grampa Banks, who snapped his heels together and pretended to salute. "Last night, there was a storm, *non*?"

Grampa Banks nodded.

"The rain most heavy, the winds most fierce?"

He nodded again.

"And the lighthouse keeper, she must tend to the light, and so she climbs the spiral stairs to the top of the tower..."

Grampa Banks was nodding almost non-stop by now.

"Then – *calamité!* – the gust of wind, it carries her over the barrier, and she falls so tragically. And yet, the constable *espéciale*, Roz Baillie, she has the eye of the detective. She sees that something in this room is not making the sense."

Grampa Banks stopped nodding and looked around the room. "What is it?"

"The fleece, *mein ami*. The fleece."

Grampa Banks squinted at the golden fleece critically. "It looks all right to me. Very nice, actually."

"*Ja, ja,*" said Bonnie. "Maude Cragge is the lighthouse keeper. She is also the Grand Maven of this Order of the Golden Fleece. She is the big boss of the island. She must tend to the light during the storm so terrible. What would she do before climbing the stairs?"

Grampa Banks thought carefully before replying. "To my mind, she'd put on her fleece."

"*Précisément!*" said Bonnie.

"Even though it is more of a parka."

Bonnie decided to ignore that.

"*Regardez*, in each photograph, we see Maude Cragge wearing the golden fleece. And yet, on the night of the torrential rain, she leaves it behind? *Impossible.*"

"Foul play?" asked Grampa Banks.

"The play most foul," replied Bonnie. "I believe that an unknown person forced the victim to climb to the top of the lighthouse last night. I am most sorry to say that Maude Cragge ... was murdered."

Bloooorororororong!

Before Bonnie's discovery had a moment to sink in, the foundations of the lighthouse were shaken with a strange sound from the clockwork mechanism. The whole structure seemed to quiver, like a tuning fork struck against a table. Picture frames rattled against the walls, and Grampa Banks had to grab the ornate balustrade to steady himself. Before Bonnie had a chance to work out what the terrific racket meant, a series of clonks came from the floorboards above.

Clonk ... clonk ... clonk.

It was the ominous tread of heavy boots approaching the spiral staircase. Someone else was in the lighthouse, and they were clonking in Bonnie's direction.

Oh no.

"We are not alone, *mein ami*!" whispered Bonnie, grabbing Grampa Banks's cardigan.

Clonk ... clonk ... clonk.

Was it the killer, returning to the scene of the crime? Was it the ghost of Maude Cragge, returning to seek revenge? Was it Iain Percival, returning to bugle Grampa Banks for a second time?

Clonk ... clonk ... clonk.

The heavy steps grew closer, and closer, until a hulking figure loomed into view on the staircase. It stooped, and an unfamiliar face glowered out of the shadows.

Chapter Four
Ribble Trouble

"Whaddya want?" rumbled a voice like a sackful of gravel in a tumble dryer.

The voice came from a barrel-chested man with a face weathered by the sun and wind. He wore a striped shirt and a weighty medallion in the shape of a white letter O. One huge hand swung by his side and the other rested on the balustrade as he stomped down the last of the stairs in steel-toed boots.

Bonnie felt as if she had woken a grizzly bear. Her first instinct was to run away, throwing lumps of meat behind her. But there was something about the man's eyes that stopped her. They were red and puffy as if this giant of a man had been ... crying.

"Summat wrong with you?" he asked gruffly. "I said: What. Do. You. Want?"

Grampa Banks looked at Bonnie. As long as she wore Montgomery Bonbon's moustache, she led the way. Bonnie let go of her grandfather's cardigan and tried to speak without her voice quavering.

"Apologies for the intrusion most rude," she began. "I am Montgomery Bonbon, the detective. This is my associate, Banks."

Click, FLASH, grrr...

Grampa Banks snapped a cheeky photo. The

assistant keeper leaned against the wall, unimpressed. "Another old boy in a cardigan, is it? Didn't you see the notice? No tours."

Old boy. Oh dear. Grampa Banks was not going to like that, thought Bonnie. You might as well have described him as a bucket full of fish bits.

"Now listen up, Sonny Jim..." began Grampa Banks. But the assistant keeper ignored him as he shoved himself off the wall and began to turn the crank handle in the centre of the room.

"No Sonny Jim here," he said eventually. "Just Reuben Ribble. I was Ms Cragge's assistant. Until the accident last night."

As Ribble turned the crank, counterweights slowly winched their way up towards the top of the lighthouse. His unusual O-shaped medallion swung from side to side. *O for ... Odde Island?* Bonnie wondered.

"I am pleased to be meeting you, Monsieur Ribble."

Reuben Ribble grunted. "Mind telling me why you're poking around my home, Detective?"

Bonnie did not want to spell out exactly why she suspected that Maude Cragge had been murdered.

For all she knew, this man himself was the killer.

So she puffed herself up, made sure that her moustache was catching the light and replied, "It is in the nature of the detective to *poke around*. Just like it is in a lighthouse keeper's nature to...?" She gestured towards the mechanism in the centre of the lighthouse.

Ribble sighed, as if about to explain something tediously obvious. "It's an old lighthouse, Mister."

"Monsieur," corrected Bonnie quickly.

"Whatever. It's like a clock. You have to wind it up to make the light turn. And every two hours you have to wind it up again. That's what the *bloooorororororong* noise is all about. A little reminder, 'cos the people who build these things reckon lighthouse keepers are all thick."

"*Ja, ja,*" said Bonnie, thinking aloud. "So last night – the night of the ... accident – the mechanism wound down and the light, it stopped?"

"So I'm told," said Ribble, straightening up. He gave a loud sniff, worthy of an elephant with hay fever, and wiped his eyes with the back of his hand. Then he turned and began to stalk slowly towards Bonnie and Grampa Banks. Before she realized it, Bonnie found herself inching backwards towards the door.

"Of course, I were on the mainland last night. Drove over to see my cousin."

Clonk.

"So I didn't see nothing."

Clonk.

"And I don't know nothing."

Clonk.

"And to be honest with you, I just want to be left alone."

Clonk.

"B-but, Monsieur," stuttered Bonnie, shuffling away from the striped shirt filling her field of vision, "Bonbon, he has the few little questions."

Clonk.

"Then Bonbon can go and ask them somewhere

else," said Ribble, opening the door widely.

Bonnie and Grampa Banks were now squeezed together in the doorway.

"We've got a tradition on Odde Island. It's called *minding yer own business*. Now, gerrout!" Ribble nodded at Grampa Banks. "You too, old boy."

"Well," said Grampa Banks indignantly, "excuse me!"

The assistant lighthouse keeper grinned. "You're excused."

SLAM!

The door rattled shut behind them.

It did not feel good to be bundled out of the crime scene so unceremoniously. Bonnie had not even had a chance to examine the top of the tower! But she had to admit that she felt glad to have a solid wooden door between her and Ribble. Like Walter Frant, the man who had tried to walk out of Widdlington Petting Zoo with two chickens in his jacket and an otter down his pants, Reuben Ribble was obviously hiding something.

The sky was darkening. The beam from Leerie Lighthouse swept over the island: cold, blue and eerily silent. On their return journey to the harbour, Bonnie and Grampa Banks heard only the sounds of nesting gulls, the sleepless churning of the ocean and the hum of Bessie's motor. Bonnie was looking forward to quietly checking into the B & B & B & B and drinking as many cups of mint tea as Grampa Banks would let her get away with.

The stars were out by the time they arrived at the guest house. It was a tall and creaky-looking building, across the road from the schoolhouse. Bonnie knew exactly what to expect from the Bright Phoebus: rooms with faded floral wallpaper and a carpet so lumpy it looked like a family of eels lived under it.

But there was something entirely unexpected on the street outside.

Grampa Banks parked Bessie in a crooked lane near by, and they were making their way towards the guest house when Bonnie spotted her. She saw a familiar head of frizzy hair, drawn back into two wild bunches.

She saw a pair of tinted spectacles that flashed and sparkled whenever the wearer had a bright idea. And finally, she saw an old-fashioned dress that even a ghost would have turned down for looking too spooky.

In short, she saw her friend Dana Hornville.

This was a disaster.

Chapter One of this book contains a lie. A blatant and inexcusable lie. Apart from Grampa Banks, there was one other person who knew Montgomery Bonbon's secret.

That person was Dana.

Earlier that summer, Dana had been of some help to Bonnie during the case of the Widdlington Eagle. Even though Dana was taller, posher and quite a bit cooler than Bonnie, they had quickly become friends.

But Dana had gone and ruined everything by working out who was underneath Montgomery Bonbon's moustache.

Since the great detective's reputation depended on keeping his true identity a secret, Bonnie was now avoiding Dana completely. Letters had been lost; telephone calls had been missed; "chance encounters" had been skilfully evaded.

And now here she was again: Dana Hornville and her mother – a tweed-wearing professor of something or other, Bonnie seemed to recall. They were walking in Bonnie's direction towards the harbourside.

To Bonnie's great relief, Dana did not seem to have spotted her – or Montgomery Bonbon – just yet.

"Well, look who it is," said Grampa Banks brightly, but Bonnie was already pulling him behind the privet hedge of the Odde schoolhouse.

"Steady on!" he grumbled, but he folded himself down next to Bonnie all the same. "You can't hide from her for ever, you know."

"Maybe I can!" whispered Bonnie, forgetting to do Montgomery Bonbon's voice.

She peered out through the spiny hedge. Dana Hornville could not have guessed that two pairs of eyes and one false moustache were watching her as she and Professor Hornville strolled by, admiring the gently bobbing boats in the harbour.

"It's OK." Bonnie breathed a sigh of relief. "She's gone round the bend."

"She's not the only one," said Grampa Banks with a sly grin.

Before Bonnie had a chance to respond, a startled squawk came from behind her. She spun round and discovered a woman in a flowery hat shoving a shapeless sack into the schoolhouse cellar. The woman stared at Bonnie and Grampa Banks with momentary alarm, then slammed the sloping door shut and padlocked it.

Bonnie knew she had to say something.

"Forgive us, Fräulein. We are ... er ... *hiding*."

The woman gave a broad smile and wiggled her eyebrows. "How exciting! Who are we hiding from?"

"From a friend," admitted Bonnie.

"Ah, yes," said the woman wisely, "I've got a few friends like that! I'm Miss Bunch; I teach here on the island."

Bonnie recognized her. She was another member of the Order of the Golden Fleece. Miss Bunch clasped her soft hands around Bonnie's and shook with such enthusiasm that Montgomery Bonbon almost lost his moustache.

"*Enchanté*. I am Montgomery Bonbon."

"Clive Banks, at your service," added Grampa Banks with a twinkle.

Miss Bunch finally stopped shaking hands, but the frills on her outfit kept quivering. Bonnie could hardly take her eyes off it.

"You like the frock? All my own handiwork," said Miss Bunch proudly, giving a little twirl before coming to a sudden halt. "Surely not *the* Montgomery Bonbon? The detective?"

"*Ja*," said Bonnie, with a modest little smile.

"Oh, Monsieuuuuur! You don't mean to tell me that there has been a – a murder? Here?"

Bonnie had not meant to tell Miss Bunch

anything at all. But the woman carried on as if she had done just that.

"My goodness, my goodness. Poor old Maude Cragge. You know, I did think it was strange..." began Miss Bunch, fluttering over to the cellar door and double-checking the padlock. "Yes, I did think it was very funny indeed," she continued, scratching her head under her flowery hat.

"Please to tell, Fräulein, what was strange and very funny indeed?"

"Well, I suppose I can tell *you*..."

The schoolteacher produced a crumpled sheet of paper from one of her many folds and frills and placed it in Bonnie's hand. It appeared to be a newsletter called the *Odde Argus*. Today's headline read:

Miss Bunch tapped the newsletter and lowered her syrupy schoolteacher's voice.

"If you do your homework, you'll find out that Lady Wallop is bound to take over as grand maven now that Maude Cragge is ... you know..."

Bonnie nodded. She knew.

"Well, it says here that Lady Wallop was at home last night when it happened. But she wasn't. In fact, I saw her ... out and about!"

"Out and – how do you say? – about?" repeated Bonnie.

"I'm sure it's nothing, of course," said Miss Bunch, shrugging as she began to walk away towards the schoolhouse entrance. "But why tell a fib about one's whereabouts on the night of a *murder*? It's just a silly notion, but I thought I ought to pop my hand up and share it with the greatest detective in England."

Bonnie winced involuntarily at the words in *England*.

Miss Bunch smiled over her shoulder. "*Bon chance*, Monsieur; goodnight, Mr Banks."

And with that, Bonnie and Grampa Banks were left alone in the schoolyard.

Studying the *Odde Argus* by the orange glimmer of the street lights, Bonnie could not help noticing something else that was strange and also very funny indeed: the schoolteacher appeared to have drawn little blue doodles all over the newsletter.

Miss Bunch's copy of the *Odde Argus* was covered with little pen drawings of *onions*.

The Odde Argus

TRAGEDY AT LEERIE LIGHTHOUSE!

BY MAANVI MALLICK, NEWSHOUND

GRAND MAVEN IN DEATH PLUNGE

Odde Island is in shock, after high winds claimed the life of lighthouse keeper Maude Cragge.

The alarm was raised at midnight by exciseman Iain Percival, when he noticed that our beloved clockwork lighthouse lantern had stopped turning. This reporter braved lashing rain and soggy sandals to join Mr Percival and schoolteacher Miss Bunch on a perilous trek from Odde Harbour across the storm-battered island.

CRAGGE'S BODY FOUND

Reaching Solan Cliffs well after 1 a.m., Ms Cragge's body was discovered at the foot of the lighthouse. It is believed that the unfortunate keeper had been performing essential maintenance on the lantern during the storm that raged from 11.30 p.m. right through the night. This tragedy comes just weeks after gales obliterated Mr Knockery's rockery.

The Argus asks: when will the nightmare end?

PAGEANT STILL ON (PHEW!)

Lady Wallop, at her home, Miserley, during the storm, was contacted this morning for comment. The Order's acting chair confirmed that the upcoming Odde Island Pageant will go ahead as a tribute to the late grand maven. A new grand maven will not be elected until after the pageant.

Chapter Five
Breakfast at Bright Phoebus

There are few things in this world more pathetic than bed and breakfast toast. Bonnie was buttering a slice so pale, so limp, so lightly toasted that you would be hard pressed not to describe it as bread. But in spite of all that, it did go quite nicely with a steaming cup of mint tea.

It was morning. Grampa Banks had joined Bonnie in her room, and he was leafing through a stack of tourist brochures and advertisements on an impractically small piecrust table.

Wrecks & Ruins: A Guide to Odde Island Landmarks

Vote Iain Percival for Grand Maven: A vote for Iain is a vote AGAINST change!

Disagreeable cat for sale: £5

Bonnie was still in bed, devouring ghost-toast and gazing out of the window. She could see Miss Bunch in her apartment above

the schoolhouse, merrily watering the flowers in a window box. The seagulls were awake, swooping and diving in the hope of nabbing an unwary breakfaster's croissant. And in the distance, morning mist and mystery clung to Leerie Lighthouse.

Roz Baillie's instincts were correct, thought Bonnie. Someone else *had* to be involved in Maude Cragge's terrible fall. Very important personages did not simply whizz off the top of lighthouses by accident. But who had helped Maude Cragge on her way? There was no sign of a break-in at the lighthouse, so it had to be someone she knew.

Reuben Ribble looked like he could easily fling someone over a railing, but he had driven to the mainland that night. Or so he claimed. Then there were the local bigwigs: the other members of the Order of the Golden Fleece. The Order seemed to be in charge of just about everything on Odde Island. Perhaps Maude Cragge's death was about *power*?

Bonnie started on a second slice of toast – corners first – and considered the suspects.

The Newshound.

Maanvi Mallick. Maude Cragge's tragic death was certainly a big story for the *Odde Argus*. Mallick was a journalist, which, Grampa Banks reminded Bonnie, meant he probably sold more porkies than a pig farmer. But did all that add up to murder?

The Aristocrat.

Who was this Lady Wallop? According to the *Odde Argus*, she was the acting chair of the Order. Acting chair might sound like something you would find in a theatre, but Grampa Banks explained it meant that she was the boss, for now. Some people would do *anything* to feel important, and Miss Bunch had seen Lady Wallop out and about on the night of the murder...

The Schoolteacher.

Then there was Miss Bunch herself. According to the *Odde Argus*, she had been with Iain

Percival and Maanvi Mallick when Maude Cragge's body was found. That seemed innocent enough, but what had she been up to in the schoolhouse cellar last night? Could Odde Island's sweet schoolteacher have a secret she was willing to kill for?

The Bloomin' Nuisance.

Iain Percival. The irksome exciseman was lucky he was not the one who'd been murdered, otherwise Montgomery Bonbon might have packed up and gone back to Widdlington. The flyer on the piecrust table told Bonnie that Mr Percival had had his eyes on the golden fleece (or parka) for quite some time. He certainly seemed to enjoy pushing people around. How did he feel about pushing people off lighthouses?

Bonnie chewed thoughtfully. The corners of the toast were gone, and she was about to attempt the middle in a single huge bite, when there came a knock at the door.

"Monsieur Bonbon? Just checking that everything is to your satisfaction?"

It was the final member of the Order of the Golden Fleece. Tobias Waterman.

Bonnie could not answer the door without her moustache, so she snuggled deeper into the bed and pulled the covers up to her nose. Grampa Banks waited for her to give him the nod, then opened the door a crack.

The Hotelier.

Tobias Waterman virtually fell into the room, as if he had been pressing his ear against the door. He tripped over a wrinkle in the carpet and almost landed on the breakfast tray. A little bowl of baked beans *splooped* onto the floor.

With one smooth movement, their host straightened up, revealing a smarmy smile.

"Oops! Still in bed I see – so sorry to intrude!"

Tobias Waterman slicked a loose lock of hair back with his palm and then wiped his fingers on a red handkerchief sticking out of the top pocket of his flashy blazer. The hotelier used so much hair product, it gave Bonnie the impression that he was wearing a greasy bicycle helmet.

"Apologies again for the mix-up at check-in. Mr Banks, I could have sworn you said one of you was under twelve on the phone."

"Nonsense," said Grampa Banks, scooping up beans.

"*C'est ridicule!*"

"And I do hope the breakfast is to your utmost satisfaction," Tobias Waterman said, examining the room very obviously.

"*Ja, ja, magnifique!*" mumbled Bonnie through the duvet. Grampa Banks made an approving humming noise.

Bonnie should have been glad of the chance to interrogate a member of the Order. But she had just spotted Montgomery Bonbon's moustache. It was where she had stuck it the night before: on the middle of the dressing table mirror. She hoped Tobias Waterman would not turn round and see it.

"You know, I didn't recognize your name last night. A little bird tells me you're a detective?"

"Correct," replied Bonnie from under the bedclothes, desperately willing her grandfather to spot the moustache before Tobias did.

"And another, much larger bird tells me you and Mr Banks visited our old lighthouse yesterday?"

"*Ja, ja,*" said Bonnie, endeavouring to catch Grampa Banks's eye and telepathically warn him about the moustache. She tried blinking an SOS. She attempted eyebrow semaphore.

"Tell me, Detective: are you treating Maude Cragge's death as ... *suspicious*?"

Mr Waterman said the word suspicious with such glee and so much saliva that he sounded like a garden sprinkler.

"Pardon me, Mr Waterman," interrupted Grampa Banks firmly, "but Montgomery Bonbon *never* comments on a case until it's solved."

"Aha! So there *is* a case to be solved? I thought so," gloated Tobias.

Grampa Banks gave Bonnie a look that said, "Sorry, old man."

She countered with a look that said, "My moustache is stuck on the mirror."

"I suppose you think Maude was murdered by someone on the island?" continued Tobias. "How thrilling!"

While Tobias was speaking, Grampa Banks began crabbing across the room behind him, towards Montgomery Bonbon's stray moustache. Bonnie knew why he was walking like a crab: he did not want to draw attention to himself. She also knew this was a mistake. The only time when it is not suspicious for someone to walk like a crab is when that person *is* a crab.

Grampa Banks was a very fine detective's assistant. But, with the best will in the world, he was no crab.

Bonnie needed to keep the hotelier distracted. She pulled the covers tight around her and attempted to fix him with a stare. Without her moustache, it was hard going.

"Perhaps you are correct, Monsieur Waterman! Perhaps there is a case to be solved. And so, *bitte*, tell to Bonbon your whereabouts on the night of the storm most dreadful?"

"This is so exciting. I've never told anyone my alibi before. I suppose I don't really have one – uh-oh!" Tobias Waterman sniggered as if it were all a big joke. "I was alone all night. The only person I spoke to was Maude Cragge herself. Important to check in with the grand maven on a daily basis – tradition, and all that."

Bonnie had to stop herself from leaping out of bed.

"You went to the lighthouse?"

"Aha ... no, Monsieur. I was downstairs in my office all night." He smirked. "On Odde Island we have things called *telephones*. They're new, but terribly popular."

Bonnie frowned, and sank back into the lumpy mattress.

"And tell to Bonbon at what time does Tobias Waterman make the telephone call, hmm?"

"Oh, I don't know..." he said, wiggling his fingers and blowing a little raspberry.

Grampa Banks was now mere inches away from the moustache. Bonnie had to keep the hotelier talking.

"Try to remember, *bitte*."

"It would have been ... around eleven. Not long before the rain started. I certainly couldn't have made it to the lighthouse in time to do her in."

With his thumb and forefinger, Grampa Banks pulled the tell-tale moustache from the mirror with a barely audible *thhhwip!*

A look of intrigue spread across Tobias Waterman's face. "Well now," he said slowly, "what is *that*?"

Bonnie squeezed her eyes closed. Had the hotelier spotted the moustache?

"IOU five hundred pounds," he read aloud.

Bonnie unsqueezed her eyes. Grampa Banks had successfully stashed Bonbon's moustache inside his cardigan. Tobias Waterman, on the other hand, was holding the scrap of paper she had found in the pocket of the golden fleece.

"Oh, I see. This must be one of your *clues*. You really are on the case, Monsieur. Well, don't let me keep you from pounding the mean streets of Odde

Harbour and whatnot."

Their host swept towards the door. Bonnie was glad to see the back of Tobias Waterman, but she did not see it for long. He turned round, one hand on the doorknob.

"You might just want to speak with Lady Wallop. Everyone knows the Wallop family doesn't have the money it used to. So sad, so sad. Of course," he added as he exited, closing the door slowly and pressing his face up to the gap, "one positively hates to gossip."

Click. Grampa Banks locked the door.

They were finally alone again. Bonnie felt the way a mouse must feel when a cat decides to wander off and be troublesome elsewhere – the guest house was quiet, but for how long?

"What do you reckon, love? The W on the IOU *could* be Lady Wallop."

Her grandfather handed her a glossy tourist brochure. It featured sepia-coloured photos of an enormous stately home named Miserley. A handful of elderly Wallops stood around looking aristocratic in front of the building's grand entrance.

"Is that where Lady Wallop lives?" asked Bonnie, spraying toast crumbs. "It's massive. Why would someone who lives *there* need to borrow money? And where was she driving on the night of the murder?"

"Only one way to find out," said Grampa Banks, jingling the keys to Bessie.

Bonnie agreed. Moments later, she was pulling on her old raincoat and digging out her beret. As she picked the cardigan fluff out of Montgomery Bonbon's moustache, she could not help thinking of Dana Hornville out there on the island somewhere, *knowing her secret.*

No. Bonnie could not allow herself to be distracted. She had a mystery to solve. Had someone done in Maude Cragge for power, or perhaps for money? If she could figure out the *why*, the *who* was bound to reveal itself.

She and Grampa Banks were soon creeping down the guest house's uneven staircase, trying not to trip over its lumpy green carpet and loose stair rods. The reception was a tiny little desk set into a wall underneath a glazed window into the hotelier's office.

Bonnie had to stand on tiptoes to see inside. The office was full of yellowing paperwork and dusty antiques, including a dubious-looking blunderbuss on the wall. Tobias Waterman was lounging in a tatty old armchair, talking away on the telephone and paying no attention to his guests.

That suited Bonnie. She did not relish the idea of a second encounter with Tobias that morning. Montgomery Bonbon and Grampa Banks were on their way to see Lady Wallop and Miserley.

Bonnie did not yet realize that the country house known as Miserley had been stolen.

Miserley House

The Order of the Golden Fleece

Grand Maven Cragge (<u>deceased</u>) — Who pushed her? <u>Why?</u>

Iain Percival (annoying) — Did he want Maude's job?

Maanvi Mallick (newshound) — What would he do for a story?

Miss Bunch (schoolteacher) — What's in the cellar?

Lady Wallop (Lady Wallop) — up to something on the night of the storm? Going for a drive?

Tobias Waterman (hotelier) — dead gossipy!

Chapter Six
Miserley is Missing

The best murders tend to happen in big old country houses. The kind of houses that have west wings and east wings, an atrium and an orrery. The kind of houses that have statues covered in dust sheets and a hidden panel in every library. The kind of houses where people display priceless vases on narrow marble columns, even though they are definitely going to get smashed.

Somehow, Bonnie had never actually solved a mystery in a big old country house. She had always wanted to. It was on her to-do list, alongside working out where Grampa Banks kept the lemon sherbets, and finding a shampoo that worked on fake moustaches.

So, it was with some excitement that she approached Miserley. Bessie crunched along a curving gravel drive, loose stones pinging and rattling off her undercarriage. It sounded like an upside-down hailstorm.

Large houses are usually surrounded by trees. This is so that the wealthy residents do not have to see any poor people. But there were no trees on Odde Island – it was too windy. So Miserley had been built up on Solan Cliffs, where rugged rocks rose up naturally above the rest of the island. Thus the Wallops of days gone by had some defence from the distressing sight of people who worked for a living.

It was only as Bessie rounded the final bend that Bonnie saw what ought to have been Miserley. She recognized the grand entrance: the huge double doors she had seen in Grampa Banks's brochure. But that was it. The long gravel drive led up to a huge doorway, standing on its own in the middle of an empty field. The rest of the building was completely gone.

Miserley was missing.

Grampa Banks was scrutinizing the map on the brochure and popping his driving glasses on and off.

"Something wrong with my specs?" he muttered. "This is where it's meant to be."

"We have come to the place most unusual, *mein ami*," said Bonnie, sliding out of the van.

The doors were made of dark and heavy oak. They had a big brass knocker in the shape of a grumpy lion eating a bagel. There did not appear to be anything else to do, so Bonnie knocked three times.

BOM—
BOM—
BOM!

There was no answer. Bonnie was beginning to feel faintly ridiculous.

"May I, old bean?" asked Grampa Banks, tucking the brochure inside his cardigan. "There's a knack with knockers."

Bonnie nodded, and Grampa Banks stepped up to the doors.

BOM-BOM-BOM!

Grampa Banks certainly had the knocker knack. The doors rattled on their hinges, and a voice from the other side answered.

"It's open!"

"Bravo, Banks," said Bonnie.

Grampa Banks beamed with the satisfaction of a job well done. He pushed the doors open for Bonnie and she stepped across the threshold.

She was not sure what she was hoping to find on the other side, and yet the sight that greeted her was utterly unexpected.

A camouflage-coloured camper van was parked in the middle of the field. Lady Wallop sat on top of it in a folding chair. She wore an ancient waxed jacket

and a pair of boots with metal spurs. A soot-stained kettle sat on a portable gas stove at her feet.

She smiled down at Bonnie and Grampa Banks serenely.

"Visitors! Marvellous!" she exclaimed, beckoning them to join her on the camper van. "Welcome to Miserley, Detective. You're just in time for tea."

Bonnie noticed the spring in Grampa Banks's step. A detective's assistant needs hot strong tea to function, and the three cups he had drunk at breakfast were obviously wearing off. Lady Wallop slung down a rope ladder, and her grandfather clambered up with more enthusiasm than was probably advisable for a man of his age. Bonnie cautiously wobbled her way up after him. The great detective was not great with heights.

Lady Wallop opened two more folding chairs with the swift crack of a lion tamer. As Bonnie and Grampa Banks sat down gingerly, she poured steaming black tea into three enamel mugs.

Bonnie had met aristocrats before. A detective could hardly cross the street without some monocle-wearing graft-dodger complaining that their pearls had been pinched. But Lady Wallop was not your regular toff; she was clearly an *eccentric*. Most aristocrats could not wait to tell you how their great-great-grandfather had won some long-forgotten battle. Looking at the heir to Miserley and her knobbly, weather-worn hands, Bonnie was ready to believe that Lady Wallop had won a fight earlier that day.

Bonnie's chair creaked underneath her. If she did not look down, it was almost comfortable. But there was an elephant in the room. Or rather, there was no elephant in the room, because there was no room at all. They were sitting on the roof of a camper van in the middle of a field. If anything, there was an elephant on the roof.

"I prefer the view from up here," said Lady Wallop by way of explanation.

Bonnie could understand why. Beyond the surrounding rocks, she could see almost the length of the island, criss-crossed with drystone walls, from Leerie Lighthouse on one side to Odde Harbour on the other. A pale smudge on the horizon might have been the causeway. A low round hill rose up in the middle of the island. A ring of thorn bushes around the treeless summit made it look like the top of a bald man's head. It was quite a view, but Bonnie could not keep ignoring the elephant on the roof.

"Please to tell," Bonnie asked at last, "what happened to your house?"

"The ex-wife got it in the divorce," said Lady Wallop, taking a big swig of tea. "Blasted lawyers, eh?"

"Mmm! Lawyers, yes." Grampa Banks nodded with all the enthusiasm of a man who does not know exactly what he is agreeing with.

Lady Wallop gave a wheeze that might just have been a posh-person version of laughter. "I'm just pulling your legs, chaps!" She stretched like an elderly cat, and settled back to tell her story.

"As a Wallop, I come from a long line of very silly people, you see. Wallop after Wallop after Wallop sold off pieces of Miserley. They didn't mean to, of course. They just gambled, borrowed, cheated and embezzled until there was nothing left. In the end, I had no choice but to get rid of it, brick by brick. A very rich American decided the whole place would look better on a golf course in Florida."

"*Ein catastrophe!*" interjected Bonnie.

"I know, *golf*!" said Lady Wallop, pretending to be sick.

Bonnie knew that one of the things a detective needed to do was establish a rapport with their suspects. That meant making them like you, so you could catch them off guard and arrest them in a more surprising way later. Like jumping out of a cake, or on waterskis.

"So sad, Fräulein Wallop, that you cannot sleep in your own home," said Bonnie.

Lady Wallop snorted. "Stuff and nonsense! I'd rather sleep here than wake up to golf balls whizzing through the breakfast room window. No, I'm a riches to rags story, and all the better for it," she concluded, draining the last of her tea.

"Come on, then, ask your questions, Detective," she added with a wry smile.

Their rapport was remaining stubbornly unestablished.

"*Pardonnez-me?*"

"You told Tobias Waterman you thought poor Maude's death wasn't an accident. The whole island is talking about it now. He cannot keep a secret, that one. So, go ahead and ask."

Bonnie took a little sip of her tea while she gathered her thoughts. It was so strong it made her eye twitch.

"Fräulein, on the night of the storm you were at home, *nes pah*?"

"Correct."

"But Montgomery Bonbon, he hears the little rumour that you were seen. Out and – how do you say? – about."

Lady Wallop shrugged. "Possible, yes. Very possible."

"But, but, but..." stammered Grampa Banks, "how in the world could you be at home *and* be out and about?"

Bonnie felt embarrassed on her assistant's behalf as Lady Wallop raised a jingling spurred boot and tapped the roof of the camper van.

Clonnnnng!

"This camper van is my home, gentlemen. It's my home here in Miserley; it's my home on Peeble Beach; it's my home in Odde Harbour. Yes, I went for a little drive, to nowhere in particular. But I certainly didn't lie about it."

"Can anyone ... corroborate this?" asked Bonnie.

"Yes, I should imagine so. Try asking the person who told you they saw me," retorted Lady Wallop, folding her arms and crossing her legs so forcefully she almost toppled off the camper van.

The interrogation was not going smoothly. Bonnie's hopes of establishing a rapport had fallen apart, like a stately home on its way to a Floridian golf course.

"But, Fräulein, is it not true that you borrow from Maude Cragge ... the money?" asked Bonnie. It was a risk to be so direct, but she had no choice.

"No, it isn't true. What would I need money for?" Lady Wallop threw her arms wide and gestured at the scenery that surrounded them.

"I see what you're thinking, Detective," she continued after a pause. "Lady Wallop has come down in the world. Maybe I bumped Maude Cragge off because I wanted to be grand maven myself?"

Lady Wallop produced a twig from her jacket pocket and used it to scratch behind her ear.

"Well, let me tell you this: my great-great – however many greats you like – grandfather founded the Order of the Golden Fleece. Thurston Wallop was a complete tyrant and an absolute fruitcake. The old villain was convinced that he would be killed by an onion, so he banned them. For good. And he made sure a Wallop would always be in charge of the Order. I was the one who changed that. Made it *democratic*, dontcha know."

"Pardon me, ma'am," asked Grampa Banks curiously, "but *did* an onion kill him in the end?"

"Of course not!" Lady Wallop scoffed. "He was crushed under a sack of turnips. But tradition is tradition on Odde Island, so the onion is still *vegetabilis non grata*. Now look here!"

Lady Wallop's laid-back demeanour had evaporated. She spoke with such conviction that Grampa Banks drank his tea with quivering hands.

"If I'd wanted that blasted fleece, I would be wearing it right now. I'm not, and I am the happiest woman on Odde Island. I have a wonderful home and good friends. Suffice it to say," she concluded grandly, "there's nothing Maude Cragge had that I wanted. So there!"

Lady Wallop went to drink from her mug, but it was empty.

"Anyone for another cup of the good stuff?"

Chapter Seven
A Dead Letterbox

As Bessie crunched down the driveway away from Miserley, Bonnie was peeling her moustache off in frustration.

That was what the note said. Tobias Waterman had suggested that W might be Lady Wallop. Now Bonnie thought about it more clearly, she saw that it was just as likely to represent the owner of the dilapidated guest house himself. Having seen the

Bright Phoebus, Bonnie could easily believe that Mr Waterman was short on cash. She should not have let him throw Montgomery Bonbon off the scent.

"Fool!" she muttered to herself. Detectives were supposed to leap into action, not leap to conclusions.

"Don't be so hard on yourself, old chap – I mean, love," said Grampa Banks, noticing that Bonnie was tucking her moustache into her raincoat pocket. "He's a slippery catch, that Waterman. And I'm not just talking about the stuff he puts in his hair. If he did owe Maude Cragge money, that gives him a motive, doesn't it?"

It certainly did.

"And, you know, I think—"

SCREEEEEEE!

Grampa Banks's *think* quickly became a *thunk* as he hit the brakes and Bessie jolted to a halt. Bonnie wiggled taller in her seat to get a better look at whatever it was Grampa Banks had spotted up ahead.

Oh dear.

It was Dana.

The road, flanked on either side by drystone walls, rolled up and over a little hillock. And right at the top was Dana Hornville, perched cross-legged on a wooden stile. Bonnie's friend was wearing yet another dress that looked like it belonged on a haunted Victorian doll, while clouds scudded gloomily behind her. Dana could have come straight from the cover of one of the books Bonnie's mum was always reading. They all had titles like *The Blacksmith's Daughter's Hamster's Bequest*, and were about young heroines, terrible uncles and poorly lit staircases.

Bonnie's first instinct was to hide: to shimmy down into the footwell and live there as a puddle of some kind. But it was too late. She saw Dana's head turn and her friend's eyes narrow. Whenever Dana squinted, her tinted glasses seemed to squint along with her.

They had been spotted. With a large grey ice-cream cone on her roof, Bessie was not the most incognito of vehicles. The country lane was too narrow to ask Grampa Banks to attempt a U-turn. They would have ended up wedged in a ditch, or knocking over a drystone wall. No. Bonnie had no option but to confront Dana. She had to nip this problem in the bud.

She needed to grasp this particular nettle. She knew that every rose had a thorn, and she...

And she...

And she was still trying to turn into a puddle when Dana knocked on the passenger window.

Knock, knock, knock!

"Bonnie Montgomery! On Odde Island, of all places," said Dana. "I say, this is a surprise."

You can tell when a posh person is about to say something, because they tend to say, "I say!" first.

Dana cocked her head to one side and gave Bonnie a wry smile. "You know, I had almost come to the conclusion that you were avoiding me."

"Really?" squeaked Bonnie, wriggling awkwardly out of Montgomery Bonbon's raincoat. Her palms were sweaty, her limbs had gone all wobbly and her brain felt like it wanted to escape through a hatch and go unicycling.

"Yes, *really*," said Dana. "After all, you did manage to miss my calls. And my letters. And my carrier pigeon."

Bonnie had forgotten about the carrier pigeon.

"You didn't even respond to my singing telegram."

"You never sent a singing telegram!" said Bonnie, without thinking.

"Aha!" said Dana triumphantly. "So you *did* get my other messages, then?"

Montgomery Bonbon was rarely lost for words, but now Bonnie found her mouth opening and closing without making a sound. She felt like a goldfish.

"And you must be the famous Mr Banks," added Dana, effortlessly sliding a business card through the open passenger window to Bonnie's grampa.

It read:

"We've taken a little cottage on the island, just for the half term," explained Dana.

Bonnie had not realized that cottages were the kind of thing people could *take*. Cottages had always struck Bonnie as a leave-them-where-they-are kind of deal.

Grampa Banks studied the card with some perplexity. "Thank you, Dana. Please, call me Clive," he said at last.

"I certainly shall, Mr Banks," said Dana. "Now, Bonnie, you must tell me ... will *he* be making an appearance?"

Bonnie's mouth opened and closed again. She felt like a goldfish who, through a series of misadventures, had found itself doing a spelling bee.

"Erm ... will *who* be making an appearance?" asked Grampa Banks, playing dumb.

"You know who I mean!" She looked at Bonnie over the top of her tinted glasses, conspiratorially. "The monsieur!"

Bonnie felt like a goldfish doing a spelling bee who had just been given the word *manoeuvre*. She wanted to explain. She wanted to apologize. She wanted to say *something*.

Instead, a little way down the road, a human head popped up out of the ground.

"I say! It's a dead letterbox."

There are not many situations that are improved by a human head popping up out of the ground, but this was one of them.

"Most curious indeed," said the head, also wearing a pair of tinted spectacles.

Dana smiled. "You haven't met Mother, have you?"

Bonnie and Grampa Banks piled out of Bessie and followed Dana. She led them a short way off the road, where the grassy bank sloped down towards the drystone wall. There they found Dana's mother crouched at the bottom of a tiny little ditch. Hunched inside it, she was almost entirely concealed behind a mass of rusty bracken.

"Mother, I would like to introduce Bonnie Montgomery and Mr Banks," said Dana.

Professor Rita Hornville looked up from the ditch. She frowned at Bonnie as if she had never seen a human being before and was not sure what you were supposed to do with them.

Bonnie attempted a greeting. "Nice to meet you, Professor Hornville," she hazarded.

"Please," replied Dana's mother at last, clambering out of the ditch and brushing dirt from her tweeds, "call me Professor Hornville."

Bonnie held out her hand politely for a shake that never came. Instead Professor Hornville pulled a large and unusually sticky snail from her knee. She dropped it unceremoniously and continued talking.

"As you can see, it's certainly not the work of local fauna. Look there, Dana, see the tool marks on the stone? This hole was made by someone on the island."

"Mother is an anthropologist," explained Dana with undisguised pride.

Bonnie had never seen anyone anthropologize before. As the professor combed through the ferns around the hole, Bonnie could not help noticing that being an anthropologist looked a little bit like being a detective.

"As I was saying, I think this *is* or *was* – or for that matter *will be* – a dead letterbox: a secret spot where messages might be exchanged – including ones about local rituals."

First a murdered lighthouse keeper, now a dead letterbox? Bonnie half expected to see a trail of distressed envelopes and wounded stamps.

"The customs and folk practices on Odde Island are singular. *Quite* singular," continued Professor Hornville, as if she were addressing a roomful of students instead of two schoolgirls and a smartly dressed former ice-cream vendor. "Notice the symbol of a ring, marking this spot as one of great importance."

The Professor was right. Around the rim of the hole, several chunks of milky white quartz formed a perfect circle.

Click, FLASH, grrr…

As Grampa Banks's camera lit up the ditch, it sparked something in Bonnie's memory.

"I've seen that before," Bonnie said aloud, before she could stop herself. Yes, she had seen a white circle the day before – but where?

Professor Hornville straightened up and stretched in a way that made her back go crick.

"I'm not surprised the shape is familiar," said Professor Hornville, obviously delighted to have a receptive audience for her lecture. "The white ring emblem is dotted around all over the island. But the locals are very cagey about its meaning, very cagey indeed." She scowled a little behind her tinted glasses. "They regard mainlanders like us as blundering interlopers. Think we're *rude*."

"Maybe—"

"All right." Professor Hornville clapped her hands together. "Off we go!"

It had been decided that Bonnie and Grampa Banks would give the Hornvilles a lift back to Odde Harbour. Bonnie did not actually remember Grampa Banks offering, but Professor Hornville seemed ever so confident. And it seemed that as long as Rita Hornville was talking, Dana was not. Bonnie had never seen her friend stay quiet for so long. And as long as Dana kept silent, she could not blurt out Montgomery Bonbon's secret. That suited Bonnie just fine.

As they all squeezed into Bessie, Bonnie's mind kept drifting back to one small detail about the dead letterbox: it had not been *completely* empty. Apart from the snail, still grumpy about having been evicted from Professor Hornville's trousers, the hole contained what Bonnie initially had assumed were scraps of paper. Or yellowed parchment. Or pieces of a crumbly old scroll.

In fact, at the bottom of the hole, she had seen a scattering of *onion skins*. Was someone sneaking shipments of onions past exciseman Iain Percival?

What a strange place, reflected Bonnie as they headed towards the harbour. She had a queasy feeling that she would not be able to solve the Leerie Lighthouse murder until she had unravelled all of Odde Island's mysteries.

Why had Tobias Waterman tried to mislead her with a story about Lady Wallop needing money?

Who was leaving onions in Professor Hornville's dead letterbox?

And the biggest mystery of all: who had pushed Maude Cragge?

Bonnie had no idea that yet another mystery was waiting for her back at the Bright Phoebus guest house.

Chapter Eight
An Unexpected Departure

The foyer of the Bright Phoebus was very still. Clocks showing the time of day in Istanbul, Paris, New York and Odde Harbour tick-tocked, ever so faintly.

As Bonnie stepped through the front door, a strange quiet pressed down on her. She was dressed in full orchestration once again: beret, coat and 'tache. Tobias Waterman would surely be keen to hear whatever gossip his guests had picked up. But he would be expecting to see Grampa Banks accompanied by a bewhiskered sleuth, not a clean-shaven ten-year-old girl.

And yet, something was wrong. Bonnie could tell that Grampa Banks had noticed it too. He walked a little closer to her, protectively.

In Bonnie's presence, Tobias Waterman had not stopped nattering for a minute, either to his guests or on the telephone. But now there was no sound of chatter coming from the reception desk. No keys were jingling. No floorboards were creaking.

Bonnie recognized the kind of silence that filled the guest house. It was the silence a cat generates just before it pounces. It was the most serious sort of silence a detective could encounter: a *deathly* silence. The air was thick with it.

She had been eager to confront the wily Mr Waterman, but as the reception desk came into view, Bonnie felt only dread. She was glad to have Montgomery Bonbon's moustache to steady her nerves, but still she found herself taking Grampa Banks's hand when he offered it.

"Must we look?" asked Grampa Banks.

"We must, *mein ami*," said Bonnie solemnly.

They peered over the desk into the quirky little office room. There, Bonnie saw Tobias Waterman, stretched out on the threadbare green carpet.

Still.

Dead.

Bonnie knew that her grandfather was a man with a heart full of compassion. Had he been a poet, he might have chosen a few soulful words to express the shock and sorrow of seeing Tobias Waterman lying there. But he was not a poet. He was a retired ice-cream vendor.

So he said, "Flamin' Nora! Not another one."

Bonnie drew herself up on tiptoes, hoping in vain to see movement on the other side of the hatch. With fingers grasping the reception desk tightly, she called out, *"Bonjour?* Monsieur?"

No response. What had she been expecting?

Tobias Waterman was sprawled on the floor, his greasy hair all mussed up. He did not look like a man in the middle of a power nap. A vintage blunderbuss, the one Bonnie had noticed the day before, lay gleaming on the carpet by his head.

The words *murder weapon* popped into Bonnie's brain – uninvited and unwelcome, like her Uncle Stanley on New Year's Eve. Everything about the blunderbuss was wrong.

Tobias Waterman, the man Bonnie had been cursing under her breath a few hours ago, was dead. And dead before she had a chance to ask him about the money he owed to Maude Cragge. Bonnie had been looking into a white O, when she was supposed to be investigating a W in the red.

She took a deep breath and tried to think clearly. There was only one way into the office: a door which had the word PRIVATE stencilled on frosted glass.

"The door," said Bonnie, darting around a corner towards it. She did not have to tell Grampa Banks to follow close behind.

"Allow me," he said, turning the handle. It rattled, but the door did not open. "Drat! Locked tight."

He tried the handle again. He barged the door with his shoulder.

Rattle, rattle, **WHUMP!**

The frosted pane of glass shivered in its setting, but the door did not budge.

"What do we do?" asked Grampa Banks.

Crashing through doors was hardly suitable work for a detective's assistant. And Bonnie herself was better at solving break-ins than causing them. She thought about using the hotel phone, but it was locked away on the other side of the office door.

"We must get help," she said, with determination.

She and Grampa Banks hurried out into the street. As soon as they emerged from the deathly silence of the guest house, the welcome sounds of island life returned: the harbour bell tolling; the locals bickering; some puffins dive-bombing a vicar.

"Regardez!"

At the far end of the street, Bonnie spotted a familiar plumed helmet. Especial Constable Roz Baillie was engaged in a heated debate with a group of Oddities about whether the triangles on bunting were supposed to point up or down. She seemed glad to be interrupted.

"I'm telling you, they go *down*, because— Can I help you, sir?"

"Tobias ... Waterman..." wheezed a slightly out-of-breath Grampa Banks. "Dead."

While gasps passed between the assembled Oddities, one face among them lit up. Bonnie had seen it before, but only in black and white: a man with eyes as sharp as the pencil behind his ear. Wearing a buff-coloured fedora, he loped over towards Bonnie.

"Maanvi Mallick, *Odde Argus*," the man said, flicking open a notebook. "I dig the dirt and print the facts. The facts, and a little bit extra! Montgomery Bonbon, is it? I recognize the face-fuzz."

"Face … fuzz?" mumbled Bonnie. She tried to wiggle her moustache authoritatively, but Maanvi Mallick had got her too flustered. He took her by the arm and marched her back towards the Bright Phoebus.

"Tell me, Monty old pal, how is poor Toby? Dead, you say? How'd it happen? Who did the deed? Keeping schtum, are you? Not surprised. Bit embarrassing for you, isn't it? Two deaths on the same island, this one right under your moustache? Care to explain yourself to my readership, Detective?"

Before Bonnie had a chance to tell Maanvi Mallick exactly how far he could fling his readership, Grampa Banks intervened.

"'Scuse me, please," he said, placing a reassuring hand on Bonnie's shoulder. "Montgomery Bonbon *never* comments on a case until it's solved."

"I've heard that before," said Mallick, licking the tip of his pencil. "Clive Banks of Widdlington? Sixty-three-year-old grandfather of one? Nice camera. You get me a couple of snaps of the stiff and I'll print 'em. No pay, but it'd be great exposure."

The newspaperman laughed as if he had told a joke.

"That's enough, Maanvi," said Roz Baillie, solemnly elbowing her way through the small crowd that was forming outside the guest house.

"Just doing my job." The reporter grinned, playfully jabbing Grampa Banks with his elbow. "She's as bad as old Craggy. Let's hope the next grand maven understands the value of a free press, eh?"

"This way, old man," said Grampa Banks, leading Bonnie up the steps and scowling back at Maanvi Mallick.

"Tell me, Monsieur, do we have a ... *murderer* on Odde Island?" called the reporter, and the little crowd quavered at the word.

Bonnie paused on the top step and turned. She knew that Montgomery Bonbon needed to say something reassuringly wise and cryptic or the newshound would never stop dogging her. She thrust her hands into her raincoat pockets and puffed up her moustache like the feathers of a bird.

"Murderers," began Bonnie, without knowing where she was going, "are being like..."

She racked her brain for something pithy to say. In the depths of her raincoat pocket, her fingers closed round a long-forgotten lemon sherbet.

"...like lemon sherbets!" she continued, whipping out the fluff-encrusted sweet and holding it aloft.

The crowd held its breath. The graphite tip of Maanvi Mallick's pencil hovered one micron above his notebook.

Grampa Banks frowned nervously. "Er ... how are murderers like lemon sherbets?" he whispered.

Inspiration struck Bonnie. She tossed the lemon sherbet towards Mallick. The newspaperman fumbled it catastrophically and it plopped into a barrel full of rainwater.

"They are being easier to catch when one is not ... *distracted*!" said Bonnie triumphantly.

Bonnie allowed Grampa Banks to lead her back inside the Bright Phoebus. Mallick called after her, his voice blending into the hubbub. "Can I quote you on that?"

The guest house door swung softly closed. The deathly silence returned.

Bonnie guided Especial Constable Baillie to the PRIVATE office door, and Roz burst it open with a single kick. Grampa Banks was more than impressed.

The office door swung loose on its hinges. And there, in front of Bonnie, was the body of Tobias Waterman, again. Roz crouched down to check for a pulse ... and shook her head sadly.

Bonnie's intuition was correct. Tobias Waterman was dead.

Bonnie had certainly not warmed to the man, but that did not give his death any less gravity. Perhaps, as an enthusiastic gossip, it would have pleased Tobias to be the talk of the island himself. A small consolation, she thought.

"Well, Detective ... Bonbon, did you say it was?" Roz asked with a tremble in her voice. "It looks to me like this old-fashioned gun thingy came loose off the wall and clonked him on the head."

Bonnie looked around the room, from inside this time: a tiny office, crammed with cobwebbed antiques. Mr Waterman lay on his back, next to his polished blunderbuss. Near by, a brass door bolt lay twisted on the carpet. Splinters on the frame showed the place where it had been wrenched out of the wood. So, Bonnie thought, the door must have been bolted from the inside when they had tried to open it.

Bonnie saw Roz Baillie make the same connection.

"So, it was locked from the inside," said Roz. "Poor man. Such awful luck!"

Bonnie could tell that the especial constable had never encountered something like this before. Roz would be more used to dealing with people who had eaten too many toffee apples and been sick in their neighbours' hats. Not dead bodies.

"Tell to me, please," asked Bonnie, "you believe the death of Tobias Waterman, it was the accident, *non*?"

"Well, the door was locked before I kicked it down. So ... it must have been an accident," said Roz. She wore the expression of a vole who has started a fight with a great white shark: out of her depth, but ready to give it a good go.

"No doubt about it," agreed Grampa Banks. "A terrible accident, wouldn't you say, old man?"

"I am afraid not, *mein amis*," said Bonnie ruefully. "Tobias Waterman was most certainly murdered."

"But-but-but how?!" asked Grampa Banks, wide-eyed.

That was the problem. Bonnie had no idea.

Kitchen + Back door

Dining Room

stairs

Reception window

Frosty window

office

Replica Blunderbuss

Hall

Visitors Lounge

Porch

The Order of Golden Fleece

Grand Maven Cragge (deceased). who pushed her? **Why?**

Iain Percival (annoying) – Did he want Maude's job?

Maanvi Mallick (newshound) – what would he do for a story? what wouldn't he do?

Miss Bunch (schoolteacher) – what's in the cellar?

Lady Wallop (Lady Wallop) – up to something on the night of the storm? Going for a drive?

Tobias Waterman (hotelier) – ~~dead gossipy!~~ dead **DEAD!**

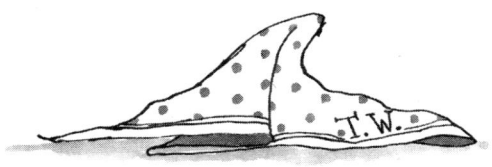

Chapter Nine
An Impossible Blunderbuss

"Murdered?"

The crime scene had grown even gloomier as the day had worn on. In this light, Tobias Waterman's junkshop antiques were actually starting to look expensive. The walls were dotted with old photographs of Odde Island, faded to blue. Tobias Waterman appeared in a dozen of them, sporting his slicked-back hair and phoney smile in every single one.

Especial Constable Roz Baillie paced in and out of the little office room, chewing a fingernail nervously.

"Murdered?" repeated Roz for the eleventyhundredth time. "It just isn't possible. It's not even a real gun. It's a replica."

Copperplate lettering on the blunderbuss's wooden mount confirmed that it was merely a decorative reproduction. Grampa Banks snapped a picture for Bonnie's records.

Click, FLASH, grrr...

"You see? It's not a murder weapon," said the especial constable, "just an ornament."

"Perhaps it is being both, *non*?" suggested Bonnie. "Tell to me, Constable *Espéciale*, what are you noticing about the victim's jacket pocket?"

Roz squinted at Tobias Waterman's once-fashionable jacket. She checked the little black notebook she carried in her own pocket. Finally she replied, "Nothing, Monsieur."

"*Exactamente!*" Bonnie clapped her hands. "*Rien!* And yet, Tobias Waterman, he wore a red handkerchief in the pocket of his jacket this morning. Where has it gone?"

Roz looked even more confused. She glanced at Grampa Banks, and he gave her a don't-ask-me shrug.

Bonnie pressed on.

"The antique blunderbuss, what does she tell you?"

"Well, erm..." Roz swallowed like someone who has just woken up to find themselves in a maths exam. "It doesn't tell me anything either. No marks, no nothing. I can't even see any fingerprints."

"*Précisément!*" Bonnie clapped twice. "Again, *rien*. Not one drop of blood. Not a smear of the slime the hotelier wears so thickly in his hair. Not a speckle of the dust which covers each and every item in this room. Do you see, Constable *Espéciale* Baillie?"

"Ooh!" Roz's eyes opened wide, and she dropped down onto a velvet footstool. "I see. I see, Detective. You reckon someone whacked him with the blunderbuss ... then nicked his handkerchief and cleaned off the fingerprints so that we would think it was an accident. Very clever!"

"Ingenious!" agreed Grampa Banks.

Bonnie rewarded Roz Baillie with the briefest of smiles and a neat wiggle of her moustache. The especial constable was clearly not cut out for police work. She was far too smart. This kind of deduction would have made Roz very unpopular among the coppers on the mainland. Bonnie's old rival, Inspector Sands, was deeply suspicious of *thinkers*. She classed thinkers alongside loiterers, ne'er-do-wells and people who played ball games on little grass triangles. In Inspector Sands's view, thinkers were not exactly criminals, but they might as well be.

"But hold on a minute." Roz stood up again. "The door was locked – latched – bolted."

Bonnie had to agree.

"So, Mr Waterman couldn't have been murdered or the killer would still be here."

All three of them froze for a moment and swivelled their eyes around the room. A chill draught seemed to pass through the guest house.

No.

No, they had examined the office from top to bottom. No murderer was crouching behind the tatty armchair. No assassin was hiding under the desk. No killer was swinging from the light fitting. And no one could have slipped out through the front or back of the guest house while all three of them were present.

When Roz had kicked the door open, the room really had been empty. Apart from the late Tobias Waterman.

"You almost had me going for a minute, Detective," said Roz with an unconvincing smile, "but it has to be a tragic accident."

"A *second* tragic accident," corrected Bonnie.

The especial constable gnawed on the end of her pencil like a woman who had wandered through the desert for a week, intensely craving the taste of an eraser. Eventually, she gave a sigh of resignation.

"All right, you win."

Bonnie closed her eyes and smiled graciously.

"I'll call Widdlington Police Station," Roz said, lifting the receiver of the guest house telephone.

"*What?*" croaked Bonnie, opening one eye.

"You're right, Monsieur. If this death really is suspicious, it's time to bring out the big guns." Roz glanced awkwardly at the blunderbuss on the floor and added, "So to speak."

Bonnie opened her mouth to protest. She knew

exactly who Widdlington would send, and the last thing she needed was Inspector Sands stomping all over Montgomery Bonbon's mystery. Bonnie's moustache was bristling with agitation when Grampa Banks laid his hand on hers.

"Let's leave the especial constable to do her job, eh, old man?" he said calmly. "It'll be a day or so before they send someone, anyway. You might have cracked the case by then."

"I hope you are right, Banks," she said doubtfully. "I hope you are right."

"Hullo? This is Especial Constable Baillie calling from..." Roz checked the number on the guest house phone. "Odde Island two-six-four. Could you put me through to Widdlington Police Station, please? It's urgent."

A thought appeared to strike Roz, and she

covered the mouthpiece with her hand. "Mr Banks, where is your little granddaughter?"

"Oh! She's, um…"

Grampa Banks withdrew his hand from Bonnie's and started to search the pockets of his cardigan, as if they contained the answer to Roz's question. All he produced was Dana Hornville's business card. It gave Bonnie an idea.

"The little *Mädchen*, she is staying with a friend on the island," Bonnie said, "at the Crow Cottage."

Roz nodded. "You two might want to join her. If this really *is* a crime scene, you can't spend the night here."

Someone on the other end of the phone squawked angrily, and Roz squeezed the receiver to her ear. Bonnie and Grampa Banks looked at one another.

It seemed that they had no choice but to seek lodgings with the Hornvilles.

"Ah, hello there," said Roz. "Is that Inspector Sands? No. No, I'm not calling about your pizza."

The Bright Phoebus B & B had not proven to be a B & B & B & B after all. It took a matter of minutes for Grampa Banks to gather their essentials: toothbrushes, undergarments, moustache combs.

"Again, ma'am," continued Roz, "I'm sorry the pizza is late, but I'm not Papa Crust."

For the final time that day, Bonnie pulled open the heavy guest house door. The little crowd outside had long since dispersed.

"Well, if I see Mr Crust, I'll pass that on, but—"

They left Roz doing battle with Inspector Sands and set off for Crow Cottage.

Bonnie's mind was aswirl with the details of the case. Or rather, cases. Two members of the Order of the Golden Fleece had died two very strange deaths that were supposed to look like accidents. There had to be a connection. Who pushed Maude Cragge? Who struck Tobias Waterman?

Most bafflingly of all, how had that person walked through a locked door?

Chapter Ten
Crow Cottage

The great detective Montgomery Bonbon left the Bright Phoebus, but it was ten-year-old Bonnie Montgomery who approached Crow Cottage soon after.

The Hornvilles' holiday rental was a short distance outside the harbour. It was a small, thickly thatched building that looked out across a wild garden towards the sea. Moonlight gave the cottage the appearance of a giant mushroom sprung up from the mossy grass.

Bonnie spotted Maanvi Mallick through the window of the neighbouring bungalow. After a long day of digging dirt, he was hunched over his home printing press. The contraption shuddered away, presumably producing tomorrow's edition of the *Odde Argus*.

Grampa Banks rang the bell for Crow Cottage, and Bonnie steeled herself. In a strange way, she found Dana more intimidating than any of the crooks and creeps she had collared in her illustrious detective career.

She needed to be certain that the truth about Montgomery Bonbon was safe in Dana's hands. And she could not allow her friend's boundless self-confidence to get in the way this time. Dana always seemed to be as cool as a cucumber. Well, Bonnie told herself, when Dana opened the door, she was going to see one massive cucumber waiting outside. And Grampa Banks.

The door opened slightly, and Dana's face appeared at the crack. Bonnie barely had time to check that Dana's mother was not within earshot before the words came tumbling out.

"Youhavetopromisenottotellanyone!" she babbled, like a really hot cucumber.

"Bonnie, dear, you must slow down," said Dana.

Bonnie took a gulp of air. Grampa Banks hung back, wringing his hands anxiously.

"You have to promise," repeated Bonnie, dropping her voice to the softest whisper, *"not to tell anyone about ... the monsieur!"*

Dana clutched at her heart, as if wounded. "Bonnie, I'm your friend! You can trust me. I promise."

Dana held out her hand. Bonnie seized it and shook with great enthusiasm. It felt good to – officially – have a friend.

"There's just one condition," Dana added with a gleam in her eye. "You must tell me *everything*."

From the moment she had spotted Dana on the island, Bonnie had been anticipating an explosive confrontation. She remembered seeing the fireworks forger Flint Touchpaper escaping the scene of a crime by riding on a bootleg Catherine wheel. This was different. No sparks were flying. No one's trousers were on fire. The Dana problem had dissolved – as swiftly and as completely as Flint Touchpaper's underpants had when he had jumped into Widdlington Harbour.

Professor Hornville had been more than amenable to Bonnie Montgomery and Grampa Banks staying at Crow Cottage for a few nights. In fact, she'd hardly looked up from reading *Can You Dig It?*, Victoria Spunge's definitive guide to the holes, pits and ditches of East Yorkshire. And who could have blamed her?

Grampa Banks made himself – not quite –

comfortable on the settee, while Bonnie made up a bed on the floor of Dana's little room.

That night, by torchlight, Bonnie unfolded the mystery of Maude Cragge's fall, and the impossible assassination of Tobias Waterman. Dana took notes, while Bonnie schoofed around the room in pyjamas and socks, racking her brain for the minute details that might make sense of the strange occurrences on the island.

She was sure about only one thing: the two apparent *accidents* had to be the work of the same person. Coincidences happen all the time, but a place as small as Odde Island left no room for coincidence. If Bonnie could identify Maude Cragge's killer, she was certain that the phantom who walked through guest house walls would be revealed too.

"We should start by drawing up a timeline," Bonnie whispered, under the low-beamed ceiling. "According to the *Odde Argus*, it started to rain half an hour before the search party set out at midnight. Midnight was when the lantern stopped, so Maude Cragge must have wound the mechanism up around two hours earlier."

Dana made a note in her unsurprisingly exquisite cursive handwriting. Of course she wrote with a fountain pen.

"Now, Tobias Waterman said that he phoned the lighthouse at eleven, from the Bright Phoebus. I think he wanted to talk about *this*," said Bonnie, producing with a flourish the IOU signed with a W.

Dana nodded and jotted down another note without comment. Bonnie felt her friend was missing the significance of the phone call.

"Don't you see? We know Maude Cragge answered the phone at eleven. We know that when she fell, she wasn't wearing the golden fleece."

"Which is actually more of" – Dana leafed back through her notes – "a parka."

"That means Maude climbed to the top of the lighthouse after eleven, but *before* the storm started at eleven thirty. So, the murder must have happened within that thirty-minute *window of opportunity*."

Dana gave that piece of deduction a brief and very quiet round of applause. Bonnie felt a warm glow.

"Now we just have to check our suspects' alibis against that window of opportunity," she said. "Reuben Ribble?"

Dana shuffled the pages of notes around. "Drove to the mainland, where he stayed the night. Or so he says."

"Hmm. What about Lady Wallop?"

Shuffle, shuffle.

"Out for a drive ... *somewhere*. Spotted out and about by Miss Bunch."

Miss Bunch, now she was a funny one. Bonnie had been so distracted by Dana popping up on *Odde Island*, she had neglected to find time to answer the question: what had Miss Bunch been so keen to keep hidden in the school cellar?

"And Miss Bunch herself?" she asked.

"Miss Bunch..." said Dana, smoothing creases out of the *Odde Argus*. "Well, it looks like Iain Percival was the first to notice that the lighthouse lantern had stopped. That was at midnight. Then he met up with Miss Bunch and Maanvi Mallick and they set off from the harbour to investigate.

It takes – gosh – well over an hour to get to the lighthouse on foot. So none of them could have done Maude Cragge in and got back to Odde Harbour in time."

Dana pulled a map of Odde Island out of the note pile and continued. "Even if the murderer had driven or cycled part of the way" – she traced a route on the map, tapping the nasty-looking rocks of Solan Cliffs – "the path is too rugged to get anywhere near the lighthouse. It would still have taken the killer around two hours to get there and back."

Bonnie wrinkled her brow. "And Tobias Waterman?"

"Well, he was in the guest house at eleven making that phone call."

Bonnie felt a sinking feeling, like a wrinkly, deflating party balloon.

Dana shuffled her notes into a neat pile and yawned. "One way or another," she said, "it looks like all your suspects have an alibi for Maude Cragge's murder." She folded her arms. "Rotten luck, old pal."

Dana was right, of course. But Bonnie was not ready to give up. Lady Wallop's alibi was shakier than a folding chair on top of a camper van. And they only had Reuben Ribble's word that he was not on the island on the night of the storm. She was not beaten yet. The truth was there; Montgomery Bonbon just needed to peel back the layers of mystery obscuring it.

Bonnie stretched out on a surprisingly cosy camping roll on Dana's carpet. She should have closed her eyes right away and gone to sleep. Montgomery Bonbon's brain surely needed the rest.

Instead, she and Dana stayed awake late into the night, discussing whether or not farts were sad to be farted.

Eventually, Bonnie had fallen asleep. She ought to have dreamed about onions that night; of strange medallions; of *something* hidden in a schoolhouse cellar. In fact, she had one of those dreams where you really, really need a wee, but you can't go because you're Queen Victoria and your spacepod has no toilet.

One way or another, Bonnie's brain got the break it needed. By the time morning arrived, several loose strands had come together to form a golden thread in her mind. A golden thread that she was just about to pull on when...

It would be unfair to say that Dana shook Bonnie awake. Yes, Dana did shake Bonnie and yes, Bonnie was asleep before the shaking and awake after it.

But what woke her was the excited whisper in her ear. "I think I've got it, by Jove!"

Bonnie did not know exactly what time it was, but as far as she was concerned it was *always* too early in the morning for *by Joves*. It was easy to forget how posh Dana was.

"Got what?" murmured Bonnie, who would not normally think about solving a murder until she had drunk a cup of mint tea and eaten breakfast. She squinted crustily out of the bedroom window. The sun was coming up over the sea. It was, at least, tomorrow. The day before the Odde Island Pageant.

"Here's how the killer did it," announced Dana, gathering up Bonnie's blankets from the floor and folding them like origami. "Tobias Waterman was found inside his office, yes? And the door was bolted on the inside?"

Bonnie pulled herself up onto Dana's bed and grunted a yes.

"What if the killer bopped poor Tobias on the head and simply climbed out through the internal window into the foyer?"

Bonnie rubbed her eyes. It seemed that both of them were prepared to open, just not at the same time.

"The window is full of ... um ... glass," Bonnie replied groggily. "There's just a little hole for handing over keys. It's way too small for a person to climb through."

Dana sagged, just for a moment. Then she bounced back.

"What if they tied a piece of string to the bolt and then fed it through the hole?"

"Oh, that sort of thing never works in real life," said Bonnie, scratching vigorously behind one ear. "You couldn't bolt the door from the window unless you had, like, an extendable cyborg arm."

Dana sagged again. "I don't suppose any of our suspects have an extendable cyborg arm?" she asked.

Bonnie shook her head. Dana slumped down onto the bed next to her.

"So how *did* it happen?"

"Patience, *mein ami*," Bonnie replied with a cryptic smile.

"You don't know, do you?" said Dana, giving Bonnie a playful shove.

"Nope," replied Bonnie, hopping off the bed. "Not yet."

Dana's enthusiastic amateur sleuthing had got Bonnie's brain into gear. Inspector Sands was probably on her way to Odde Island right now and Montgomery Bonbon needed to squeeze the most out of every minute until she arrived. A golden thread was dangling in front of Bonnie. She pulled on it.

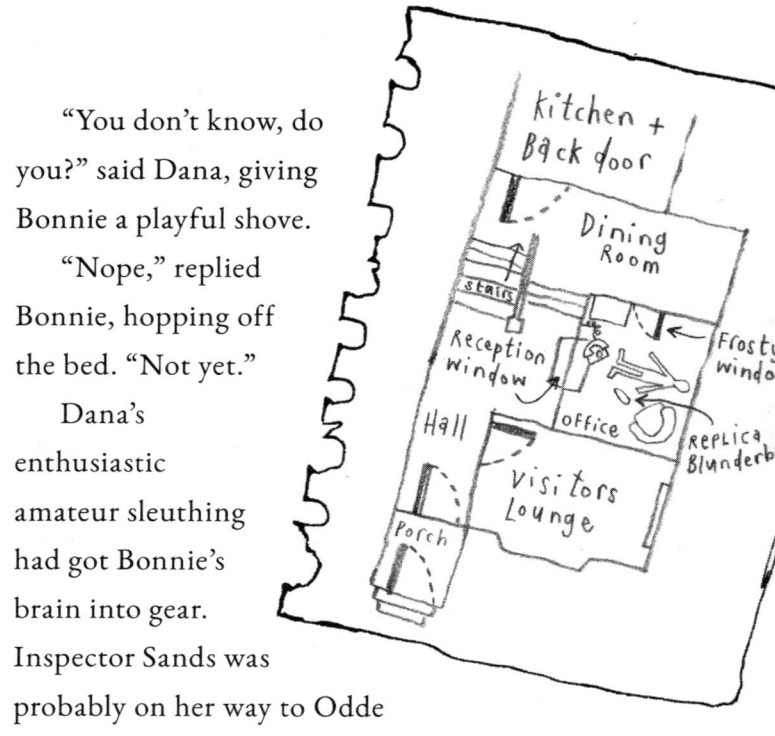

"I think we've been looking at this case the wrong way," she said, putting her shoes on.

"Bonnie dear, you're still wearing your pyjamas," Dana pointed out.

"What? Oh, right!"

Bonnie tried to get her pyjamas off without removing her shoes. She fell over.

"As I was saying," she said, wriggling about on the floor, "we've been talking about alibis when we should have been thinking about *motives*."

With a wrench, Bonnie wrestled one pyjama leg free, catapulting her left shoe across the room. Dana caught it effortlessly before it flew through the open window.

"Tobias Waterman was a gossip. Lady Wallop said he *could not* keep a secret."

"So, you think he found out something he shouldn't?" asked Dana, helpfully tugging at a miscellaneous section of pyjama.

"I think," said Bonnie, diving into a fresh set of clothes, "that Tobias Waterman stumbled onto something big: Odde Island's secret *smuggling ring*."

"A smuggling ring?" asked Dana, tossing Bonnie's left shoe roughly in the direction of a foot. "Smuggling what?"

"Onions!" Bonnie exclaimed triumphantly, standing upright. "The evidence is all over the place.

I reckon your mum's mysterious white circles are drop-off points."

"Hold on a moment," said Dana. "Didn't you say that Reuben Ribble was wearing a white ring around his neck?"

"And when I met him, he had been crying. Because of Maude Cragge's death? Or because he had been—"

"Cutting onions!" finished Dana. "Brilliant!"

"Mmm-hmm." Bonnie nodded. "What if Maude Cragge found out about her assistant's little sideline, and he had to get rid of her? And maybe Maude told Tobias Waterman before she was killed?"

"When he telephoned the lighthouse!" chipped in Dana.

"So Waterman had to go as well. And that's not all. I think I know who's behind the whole operation."

Dana seemed genuinely impressed. Bonnie savoured the moment.

"Now, come on," said Bonnie, tapping one of the funny onion doodles adorning their copy of the *Odde Argus*.

"Today we uncover ... an *onion ring*."

Timeline

11pm Tobias spoke to Maude. He was in guest house.
? Maude goes to top of lighthouse.
11.30pm Started to rain.
12am Lighthouse stops. Search party sets out. Miss Bunch, Iain Percival and Maarin Mallick meet in the harbour.

THEORIES FOR HOW TOBIAS WATERMAN COULD HAVE BEEN KILLED
BY BONNIE + Dana

Maude Cragge's **ghost**?

cyborg?

fishing line

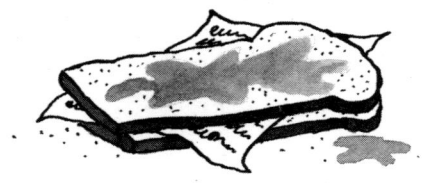

Chapter Eleven
The Bunch Hunch

Suspicions are important to a detective. Suspicions are like fuel; they keep the sleuthing engine going, churning up clues and spitting out deductions. A good detective can be suspicious of absolutely anything: a box of chocolates, a bouquet of flowers, an adorable kitten.

The box of chocolates? *Probably poisoned.*

The vase of flowers? *Probably bugged.*

The adorable kitten? *Evil. Just look at it.*

But, as important as they are, suspicions are not enough on their own. Before a detective can cry, "*J'accuse!*" she needs hard evidence. Bonnie needed to find proof before she started throwing around j'accusations. This meant she needed a plan.

Grampa Banks would be delighted at the prospect, she thought. He enjoyed a good plan; he savoured a scheme; he relished a ruse; he even partook in a wheeze, now and again. Bonnie's grandfather–slash–assistant preferred to know exactly what was going to happen and exactly when it was going to happen. That was not Bonnie's style. She liked to rely on her instinct, her intuition and, most disgustingly of all, her gut.

But that morning, she had no choice. She was experienced at being two people at once, but she could not be in two *places* at once.

A note, concealed between slices of toast, was slipped to Grampa Banks across the Crow Cottage breakfast table. This went unnoticed by Rita Hornville. The professor merely sipped her coffee and read aloud from *Odde Folk* (1953) by Warburton Hamm-Sandwich.

Grampa Banks surreptitiously unfolded the warm buttery note. He read it, and gave Bonnie a deliberate, over-the-top wink. The plan was *go*.

Bonnie needed Dana's help to break Reuben Ribble's alibi for the night of the storm. Meanwhile, Grampa Banks would do what he did best: the boring stuff. Someone with a set of wheels had to check up on the various suspects' whereabouts during Tobias Waterman's murder. Odde Harbour had been busy yesterday in the lead-up to the pageant – had anyone been spotted lurking around the guest house? Were any of the suspects unaccounted for at the time of the hotelier's *early check-out*? Clive Banks was on a mission to find out.

If today went to plan, Bonnie would be able to prove that Ribble had been lying about being off the island on the night of Maude Cragge's death, and that he was in cahoots with the mastermind behind the entire onion operation: Miss Bunch.

"Miss Bunch! How ever did you work out she was behind it?" asked Dana, as soon as they were alone together on the footpath leading to Odde Harbour. Dana was far too cool to sound flustered, but Bonnie thought she detected a hint of flusteration in her friend's voice.

"Call it a hunch," said Bonnie. "A Bunch hunch. The evening before Tobias was murdered, I bumped into her in the schoolyard when you ... I mean, when I..."

Dana did not need to know about Bonnie hiding from her behind a hedge, did she?

"The point is, I caught her stuffing a sack of something into the schoolhouse cellar. You saw her doodles – she's got onions on the brain. I think Reuben Ribble smuggles the onions onto the island, and Miss Bunch stores them underneath the schoolhouse. It probably stinks down there. I bet that's what the white circle represents – the onion ring."

"I've never met an actual smuggler before," said Dana. "Remember, if things get rough, I was the Saint Heriburga's fencing champion two years in a row. Do you fence at all?"

Bonnie had no idea how you would even begin to use a fence in a fight. Perhaps you would try to get your opponent onto the pointy bits? Or put up a *Keep Out* sign and stand behind it?

"We are going to use our brains, not our fences," she said.

"Oh, jolly good," agreed Dana, adjusting her tinted spectacles. "So, where are we going?"

They were going undercover. Two girls could move around more inconspicuously than a renowned detective.

Bonnie had had no idea what an exciseman was before she came to Odde Island. Now she understood that an exciseman's job was to be absolutely as irritating as possible, all the time. Exciseman Iain Percival, secretary-in-something to the Order of Whatever, was what Grampa Banks would describe as a jobsworth. He was a petty, pedantic pencil-pusher.

And that was exactly what Bonnie needed to catch Reuben Ribble in a lie.

She knew that Iain Percival stood constant guard in the little building called Excise House at the end of Odde Causeway, sticking his nose anywhere it would fit and trying to sniff out contraband. The unusual geography of Odde Island meant that there was only one way on and off the island by road: across the causeway when the tide was out. So, if Ribble really had driven to the mainland on the evening of the storm, Exciseman Percival would definitely know about it.

Bonnie needed to sneak a look at Iain Percival's records, and Montgomery Bonbon was not the right man for the job. Iain Percival simply *lived* to inconvenience visitors to the island. Better to try and catch him unawares.

"The Usual Strategy?" asked Bonnie.

Dana glanced at her quizzically over her glasses. "I beg your pardon?"

"Oh, right!" Bonnie was so used to investigating with Grampa Banks she had forgotten that Dana was new to the detecting lark. "I mean, you keep Mr Percival talking and I'll pretend to pop to the toilet and ... you know ... snoop around."

Maybe this was going to be trickier than she had anticipated. If she had brought Grampa Banks, he could have distracted Mr Percival with Old Man Chat. They could have had a long pointless chinwag about fishing, or cardigans, or the best way to get from one place to another.

But then Dana would have had to drive Bessie. And this case did not need the Hornville girl flinging fences at the other suspects.

"Keep Mr Percival talking. Roger that," agreed Dana. "I'm good at talking."

That is true, thought Bonnie. It runs in the family.

"But hang on a mo. How do we know we can trust Mr Percival's records?" asked Dana shrewdly. "He is a suspect, after all."

Bonnie had the feeling Iain Percival would rather eat a raw onion than falsify an official document. But Dana had a point. The exciseman had a very good motive for getting Maude Cragge out of the way: he wanted to be grand maven himself.

"I think," said Bonnie carefully, "that we can kill two birds with one stone."

She did not mean that literally. That would be revolting. She meant that they could take the opportunity to nose around Iain Percival's records *and* suss out the man himself. Was he capable of murdering more than a packet of crisps?

When they reached Excise House, Iain Percival was haranguing a cyclist who was travelling with a tin of leek and potato soup in her rucksack. Leeks are not technically onions and potatoes are definitely potatoes. So, in the end, the exciseman had to let the visitor off with a stern warning.

Bonnie clasped her hands behind her back and squeezed nervously. Dana hurried up the wooden steps towards Mr Percival just as he was reaching the door to his little dwelling.

The plan was go.

"I say! Exciseman Percival?" she called out.

Iain Percival swung round, clinging on to his clipboard with both hands.

"Yes, what?" he barked, the tiny tuft of hair on his head wafting like a flag stuck in a big bald island. "Oh, it's you. The little Hornville, is it?"

"Dana," said Dana, "and this is my friend Bonnie."

Bonnie scurried up behind Dana and tried to smile like a convincing ten-year-old girl.

"Miss Cheese and Onion Crunchy Puffs," said Mr Percival drily.

"Bonnie has been ... er ... caught short," Dana continued. (Surely there was a better phrase for needing a wee than that? Bonnie wondered.) "Could she, by any chance, use your loo?"

Mr Percival shook his quiff. Nothing with this man was going to be straightforward. He took one of his very deep breaths.

"Offcomers MAY not lay claim TO the usage of any private convenience, except at the discretion OF the titleholder OF said convenience," he rattled off.

Dana thought on this for a moment. "Do you mean ... she can't use your toilet unless you say she can?"

As a posh kid, Dana had more practice than Bonnie when it came to translating pompous nonsense. Iain Percival scratched his quiff and pretended to consult his clipboard.

"Couldn't she use a public amenity?" he asked finally.

There were no other buildings in sight of Excise House. Iain Percival looked around anyway, seemingly in the hope that a public lavatory had been erected since the last time he blinked.

"I could go in the sea," said Bonnie, her voice sounding a little squeakier than she would have liked, "but I'm afraid that might be..." She cleared her throat and tried to speak louder. *"Against the rules."*

A light bulb seemed to ping on behind the exciseman's eyes.

"Quite right you are!" he spluttered. "Public nuisance IS expressly prohibited within AND furthermore utterly forbidden outwith the confines of Odde Island. Which is to say ... um..." With glum resignation, the exciseman opened the door. "You may come in."

He hurried Bonnie and Dana inside, and the door squeaked shut.

Bonnie's eyes slowly adjusted to the dark interior. It was clear that Iain Percival both worked and lived in Excise House. It had the musty smell of an old board game with missing pieces. Venetian blinds on the windows gave a clear view of Odde Causeway without letting in more than a few slivers of light.

Despite the dimness, Bonnie could see that the place was meticulously neat. Even Grampa Banks did not leave the kitchen so tidy after cooking. The walls were lined with slim cupboards and shallow drawers, each one carefully labelled. Even the spices in the spice rack were in alphabetical order. And every jar was full and unopened.

Mr Percival, Bonnie deduced, was not a man whose life had a lot of spice.

"Untidy," came a voice from somewhere in the gloom.

"Untidy? I would have said scruffy meself," said a second, almost identical voice.

Iain Percival quickly fumbled his little quiff of hair into a neat point.

"It's rather windy, Aunty. Very breezy, Uncle," called back Iain Percival. "The toilet is through my office," he whispered to Bonnie. His indoor voice was much softer than the one he used on duty. "Watch out – the seat's always cold."

"Excuses," croaked the first voice.

"Excuses indeed," agreed the second voice. "Excuses are like friends, young Iain. Making them is a total waste of time."

Chapter Twelve

Aunty and Uncle

"Good point, Aunty. Well made, Uncle," said Iain Percival automatically. Bonnie got the impression it was something he said a lot. The girls exchanged a glance. Even by the standards of Odde Island, there was something funny about this place.

"Visitors?" asked the voice which Bonnie had come to know as Aunty.

"Visitors? Who is it, Iain? What do they want?" asked the voice known as Uncle.

Iain Percival twisted his face into a weak smile and shooed the girls towards two figures seated at a little round table in one corner. Both held playing cards, but they were so still Bonnie might have mistaken them for part of the furniture. Their only colour came from an overhead light bulb and the reflection of the table's green baize. Though they spoke to Iain Percival, they did not turn their eyes away from the cards.

Bonnie blinked at them in the low light. She had thought Iain Percival looked old. If this pair had been any older, Dana's father could have stuck them in a glass case at the Hornville Museum.

"The tourist girl, she needs to use the ... ah ... smallest room," Iain Percival explained, pointing at Bonnie.

Aunty and Uncle still did not look round.

"Risky," said Aunty.

"Bit risky, lad," agreed Uncle. "Might be a murderer on the loose."

A fresh edition of the *Odde Argus* lay on the baize between the weird pair. The grisly headline screeched *Bed & Bloodbath?* Iain Percival swept up the offending newsletter and filed it away deftly in a little newspaper rack.

Bonnie marvelled. Iain Percival, who bullied everyone who set foot on the island, had turned into a meek child in front of these two creatures. Aunty and Uncle did not really suspect her and Dana of being ruthless killers. They were just looking for excuses to needle Iain.

"What's the matter, Aunty? Why so put out, Uncle?" asked Iain. "I've done all my chores, haven't I?"

"Backchat!" snapped Aunty.

"Backchatting your old aunty, Iain? The cheek of it! The impertinence!" added Uncle.

Snipes, jibes and words you cannot print in a children's book began to rain down around Iain.

Bonnie felt a tug on her hand. It was Dana, not talking for once, but wiggling her eyebrows very loudly. "Come on," they seemed to say, "while they're distracted!" She pulled Bonnie towards a door that appeared to lead to the exciseman's office.

The office was as fastidiously organized as the kitchen. From the filing cabinets to the bookshelves, everything in the room had its own label, written in Iain Percival's small, regular hand.

INFRACTIONS

MISDEMEANOURS

VIOLATIONS

The pencils on the writing desk, all sharpened to exactly the same length, had Iain's name printed on them. Even some of the labels had labels. It was enough to make Bonnie's head spin. Grampa Banks had a lot to learn about being a neat freak.

From the other room, Bonnie heard Aunty uttering the word, "Ungrateful!"

"Ungrateful is an understatement, I'd say," chimed in Uncle.

The horrible twosome was still lobbing verbal hand grenades at their nephew, but for how much longer? Bonnie needed to act fast.

"He notes everything down on that clipboard of his," she whispered to Dana. "We need his records for the evening of the storm. That's ... three nights ago."

Dana had already found a cabinet labelled *Crossings* and was pulling drawers out and noiselessly rifling through folders.

"Lazy!" came Aunty's voice.

"Lazy! Would it hurt you to tidy up once in a while?" demanded Uncle.

"But – but..." protested Iain Percival.

Dana's fingers were a blur. She flicked through the excise records with the alacrity of a concert pianist. Bonnie was about to join her, when something else caught her attention. It was a neatly bound stack of flyers, and it had been stuffed into a wastepaper basket.

Vote Iain Percival for Grand Maven
A vote for Iain is a vote AGAINST change!

The glossy mugshot of Iain Percival's face stared up at Bonnie from his own bin bottom. How strange. Bonnie could not help wondering

if Iain Percival had changed his mind about wanting to wear the golden fleece (that was actually more of a parka). But she did not wonder for long, because Dana was about to whisper in her ear.

"Got it!"

Bonnie spun round to see Dana clutching a handful of sheets with holes punched down either side of the off-white paper. When her friend spoke again, there was a nervous edge to her voice that Bonnie had never heard before.

"Look here," she said, "there's no record of Reuben Ribble popping over to the mainland on the day of Maude Cragge's death. He fibbed."

"I knew it," whispered Bonnie, taking the papers from Dana and hurriedly folding them six times.

Dana eyed the office door, warily. "This undercover business is a bit rum, wouldn't you say?"

Apart from Dana, no one born after 1906 would have said it was a *bit rum*, least of all Bonnie.

"You must be awfully brave, getting up to

perilous japes like this all the time," Dana continued, adjusting her spectacles.

At this point, Bonnie Montgomery made a mistake. She should have been like Iain Percival, and filed Dana's comment away for future reference. She should have focused on the perilous jape in hand. She should *not* have tried to act cool.

"Well, you know what they say," Bonnie said with a drawl, "detectives like me eat peril for—"

She was going to say *breakfast*. And it would have been a lie, because she actually ate toast for breakfast. But Bonnie's real mistake was leaning nonchalantly against the drawer Dana had left open. She lost her footing as the drawer slid shut with a loud...

CRACK!

Before Bonnie had time to recover from her stumble – and before she had a chance to slip the folded papers into her backpack – a sharp intake of breath at the office door froze both girls stiff.

"Mess-makers!" spat Aunty.

"Nasty little mess-makers, making a mess," repeated Uncle. They stood in the doorway, glowering at Bonnie and Dana.

Bonnie had no time to think. She grabbed Dana's hand, concealing the purloined documents between their palms.

"Out!" cried Aunty.

"Throw the trespassers out, Iain!" demanded Uncle hoarsely. "Oh, we should never have let you take over around here. No respect for tradition."

"You'd better go," said a weak voice from the kitchen behind them.

Had Aunty and Uncle actually spotted Bonnie holding the records? She was not sure, but if she let go of Dana's hand there would be no doubt about it. If she wanted to keep the stolen pages hidden, she had no choice but to walk sideways, dragging Dana like an oversized doll, between the dreadful elder Percivals, who loomed overhead like gargoyles on either side of the doorway.

Hand in hand, Bonnie and Dana crabbed a stupid crab walk out of the office and towards freedom. It would have made Grampa Banks proud.

"Slack!" complained Aunty, showing no sign of running out of steam.

"Things have got ever so slack since our day. Didn't even hear a flush! Nasty girls!"

Iain Percival did not look up as they passed him, cowering behind his relatives. He did not say anything either. He just listlessly cleaned his glasses, playing cards scattered all around. Bonnie recognized the feeling. She knew what it was like to be told off by a grown-up when you had done nothing wrong. And her cheeks still stung with the embarrassment of messing up in front of Dana.

"Good-for-nothing!" grumbled Aunty.

"You're good for absolutely nothing!" agreed Uncle. "How do you expect to be elected grand maven when you can't even keep your own house in order, eh?"

The girls were nearly at the door, when Bonnie found her feet had stopped moving of their own accord.

"Come on!" said Dana, from the corner of her mouth. She tried to shoulder-barge Bonnie towards the door, but Bonnie stood firm.

"Excuse me?" Bonnie caught herself saying.

How would Montgomery Bonbon have dealt with bullies like Aunty and Uncle? What would he have said? And what could Bonnie say, as the ten-year-old perpetrator of a very low-key heist?

Bonnie paused to make sure she had everyone's attention.

"I just wanted to say thank you to Mr Percival for letting me use the loo. He works so hard, and everyone on the island really respects what he does."

Iain Percival lifted his head. There was a look in his eyes that was new. She had not told the truth. Not exactly. But her words had set Aunty and Uncle bridling, like cats that had been stroked backwards. Bonnie's courage began to ebb away under Aunty and Uncle's combined glare.

"And I think you two should ... um..."

"Jolly well..." suggested Dana helpfully.

"I think you should *jolly well* be a little bit nicer to him. Shame on you!"

Bonnie was shocked by her own audacity. Aunty was speechless, and without her, Uncle had nothing to say.

They both looked at Iain Percival, who said quietly, "You're very welcome, girls."

He finished polishing his glasses and popped them back on his nose. "Do you know, I never really wanted to be grand maven? I just wanted to impress you, Aunty. And you, Uncle."

Aunty and Uncle seethed silently.

"Well, I've had enough of that. There's nothing

wrong with just being an exciseman, after all. And IN light of the fact that a civilian vehicle IS approaching, I must attend to my duties IN my capacity as exciseman of Odde Island."

Through the window, Bonnie could see a car curving its way across the causeway. Iain Percival grasped his clipboard and marched towards the door. He paused next to Bonnie and Dana and puffed out his chest.

"Now, Aunty and Uncle: IF you two tidy up those cards quick sharp AND promise not to throw another tantrum when I get back, I might JUST be persuaded to forgive you FOR your rudeness and then put the dinner on. Understood?"

There was a long, creaking pause.

"Understood," said Aunty, at last.

"Absolutely understood," added Uncle. "I'm ready for a bit of dinner."

Iain Percival opened the door. "After you," he said, and Bonnie and Dana tumbled outside and down the steps with all the elegance of a newborn pantomime horse.

The girls retreated from Excise House as quickly as they could. Looking back, they saw Iain Percival marching towards the red and white barrier, whistling happily in anticipation of ruining some poor tourist's holiday.

Bonnie tucked the alibi-busting evidence into her backpack, and Dana clapped her on the back.

"Standing up to those two ghouls," she said, "now *that* was brave."

Chapter Thirteen
Peeble Beach

It felt invigorating to be out in the sea air, instead of trapped inside Iain Percival's stifling home.

Seagulls swooped overhead. With truculent squawks, they informed one another where the largest parcels of chips and the weakest-looking tourists could be found. They had no interest in the detective work that had gone on in the little house below. Anyone trying to kill two of these seagulls with one stone would have been lucky to escape Odde Island with all their fingers.

Nevertheless, Bonnie's visit to Excise House *had* killed two birds with one stone. She now had proof that Reuben Ribble had lied about driving to the mainland on the night of the murder. *And* she had gained a little glimpse inside the grim world of Iain Percival.

"So, do you think he was telling the truth?" asked Dana. "About not wanting to be grand maven?"

Bonnie thought back to the bundle of flyers in Iain Percival's wastepaper basket. For the exciseman, it seemed that the golden fleece (or parka) really *had* lost its shine. But before she had a chance to put that into words, Bonnie heard the familiar *chug-chug-chug* of a former ice-cream van approaching.

"Ahoy!" called Grampa Banks as Bessie rolled to a stop by the side of the road. "There's been a *development*."

Bonnie's grandfather sprang out of the vehicle so quickly Bonnie wondered if he had installed an ejector seat. The last time she had seen him this excited was during the summer sale at Loafers 2 Go. He clearly had important news.

"I take it your investigation was a success, Mr Banks?" said Dana as they approached the van.

"An utter disaster, thank you, Dana!" replied Grampa Banks, beaming.

"Just about anyone on the island could have entered the guest house between the time we went to Miserley and the time we got back and found the body," he continued, with no less enthusiasm. "Even Lady Wallop could have got there before us, if she'd really wanted. Nope – everyone's alibi is soggier than an ice-cream sandwich in a sauna."

"So, did you find a fresh witness? Was someone seen at the guest house?" asked Bonnie, tangling with the sleeves on Montgomery Bonbon's raincoat.

"Double nope. The locals are fuzzier than an old tennis ball. With the pageant coming up, the harbour was packed. Someone told me they saw Genghis Khan picking up his dry cleaning."

There had to be a reason why Grampa Banks was so excited, thought Bonnie, sticking Montgomery Bonbon's moustache to her upper lip.

"Then please to tell, *mein ami*," she said firmly, "why have you got the little ants inside your pants?"

"Walk this way, old bean. Walk this way."

"I was about to go up to the lighthouse to grill Reuben Ribble, when I spied him climbing down the rocks," Grampa Banks explained. "He's more nimble than he looks, that one. Like a mountain goat in the body of a darts player. I followed him, surreptitious-like, keeping my distance. And he ended up ... here!"

Peeble Beach spread out ahead of Bonnie. She and Dana had followed Grampa Banks along the shore on foot. Eventually, they had reached an isolated, crescent-shaped cove, sheltered all around by cliffs. This was not the kind of beach where tourists laid out towels and deckchairs. No balls were likely to be volleyed and no sands were going to be castled here. Peeble Beach was that most dreaded of holiday destinations: a pebble beach.

It was low tide. The sea foam whispered in and fizzed out with a kind of hush. Even the seabirds seemed calmer here. They were content with barking quietly at each other, standing on one leg or tucking their beaks under their wings to find out what a seagull's armpit smells like. The beach was home to a handful of larger rocks: lumpy with barnacles or draped with hairy green algae.

"There! Look!"

Grampa Banks waggled a finger up ahead. It was not Reuben Ribble that had caught his eye: the beach appeared to be empty. But there was ... *something* ... that Bonnie had mistaken for another mossy boulder. She realised that she was squinting at a small, upturned rowing boat, camouflaged by an ancient fishing net. It was exactly the kind of secret vessel a smuggler would need to sneak onions onto Odde Island.

"Magnifico!" she said, speeding up.

"Excellent work, Mr Banks," said Dana, and he glowed with pride.

As they approached the boat, Bonnie began to realise that Peeble Beach truly was a smuggler's

dream. Sand was always ready to dob a criminal in. "You want footprints?" it said. "We got your footprints right here!" But there would be no helpful tracks today. The stones underfoot, knobbly and wobbly, seemed to say, "Come back in a thousand years. I might be sand then."

The only thing Peeble Beach appeared to be missing was a smuggler. Reuben Ribble must have concluded his business on the shore while Grampa Banks was fetching Bonnie and Dana. It would have been satisfying to catch the red-faced Ribble red-handed. But he had to have left behind *some* clue that would tie the boat to the smuggling ring, and the smuggling ring to the murders.

Grampa Banks hung back, pinching his trouser legs to keep the turn-ups out of a rockpool. Dana also seemed reluctant to get too close to the rowing boat's grimy undercarriage. Montgomery Bonbon, however, was not going to be put off.

Bonnie crouched down, her nose almost grazing the boat's wooden hull. Stinky sea-smells coiled around her as she began to circle around the vessel, searching for white rings, loose onions or any other tell-tale signs of smuggling. Only barnacles stared back at her.

She sniffed her moustache thoughtfully, then wriggled her fingers underneath the boat's gunwale. Bonnie did not know that the rim of a boat is called a gunwale. She also did not know that it is pronounced "gunnel". But that did not stop her taking hold of it and attempting ... to ... *HEAVE!*

The little boat did not move an inch.

Dana and Grampa Banks quickly joined her, straining against the weight of the boat.

HEAVE!

Bonnie could feel little stones scraping wetly against her fingertips. The salty smell of the fishing net stung her nostrils as she heaved and heaved. Dana's face was screwed up with exertion. Grampa Banks looked like he was blowing up an invisible balloon. The boat hardly budged.

Then Bonnie heard it. A yawning sound.

The pebbles of Peeble Beach were set rattling by the low moan of a creature from the deepest depths.

Suddenly, the boat Bonnie was gripping became lighter. The gunwale began to rise up and Bonnie half expected to see the tentacles of a sea beast slithering out from beneath it.

"What on earth...?" said Grampa Banks, staggering back as the boat began to rise of its own accord.

Dana pulled Bonnie away, as the rowing boat lifted to reveal a fearsome sight. It was the sun-scorched face of Reuben Ribble.

"Can't a fella have forty winks in peace?" said the assistant lighthouse keeper, pulling himself out from under the boat.

Reuben Ribble cricked and cracked the bones in his neck. He dug sleep out of one eye with a mucky fingernail. Then he stretched up, towering over Bonnie.

"Minty Beauregard. I thought I said I wanted to be left alone."

"His name is Montgomery Bonbon," corrected Dana, folding her arms.

"And who are you?" scoffed Ribble. "His

bodyguard? You look a mite tougher than the old boy in the cardigan, I'll give you that much."

"Old boy?" repeated Grampa Banks, looking like he was about to burst into flames.

"For your information, Mr Ribble," said Dana, coldly, "I happen to be a fencing champion."

"Oh yeah?" grinned Ribble. "Well, I'm a dab hand at putting up a shed. Now is anyone going to tell me why Mr Detective is poking around my private property?"

Bonnie cleared her throat, quietly.

"The boat, she does belong to you, *nes pah*?"

Reuben Ribble crunched a step towards her and placed his hands on his hips.

"So what if she does? What business is it of yours if I have a little nap when I'm working on my boat?"

Bonnie crunched a step towards Ribble and placed her own hands on her own hips.

"Crime, Monsieur," she said, with a moustache wiggle. "Crime is my business. And you, Reuben Ribble, are being a criminal, a crook and a *contrabandista*!"

"Codswallop!"

"Tell to Bonbon: the medallion you wear around your neck, is that not the symbol of Odde Island's secret smuggling ring?"

Bonnie watched Reuben Ribble's smile flicker and fade. He hesitated, fingers tickling at the medallion. She could see his mind working, like the mechanism at the heart of Leerie Lighthouse. At last, he spoke.

"All right. What do you know?"

Bonnie had not expected to be j'accusing Reuben Ribble this soon. She knew that she was not ready. She just had to hope that Reuben Ribble did not know.

"Firstly," said Bonnie, trying to sound confident, "you lied to Bonbon about driving to the mainland on the night of the storm. Secondly, Bonbon knows that you are smuggling the onions and you do not work alone. Your accomplice, she aids you in the distribution of the ... forbidden fruit."

Reuben Ribble said nothing, wiping a hand across his top lip. Was he sweating?

"Thirdly and most shamefully," Bonnie pressed

her advantage, "when Maude Cragge uncovers your little *projekt* ... you push her from the top of Leerie Lighthouse."

She had said it. It felt like rolling the dice in a game of snakes and ladders. Reuben Ribble stood motionless, like a statue carved out of ham. Then, very gradually, his smile returned. It crept across his lips, from one corner to the other until he was grinning broadly.

"You reckon I killed old Maude? Oh dear, oh dear!" said Reuben Ribble, apparently enjoying himself. "If that *is* what you think, then you're taking an awfully big risk, aren't you? Confronting a cold-blooded murderer in the middle of nowhere? Doesn't seem wise to me."

It did not seem wise to Bonnie either, but she stood her ground. She felt Dana and Grampa Banks draw close on either side. Dana clenched her fists. Grampa Banks muttered, "Old boy?" under his breath.

"Tell you what, Mr Detective, answer me one question," said Reuben Ribble.

He crouched down and looked Bonnie dead in the eye.

"Have you ever tasted Odde Onion Stew?"

Chapter Fourteen
The Onion Ring

Reuben Ribble walked ahead, easily taking the humps and bumps of the clifftop path in his stride. Bonnie was a few steps behind, scrabbling to keep up with her suspect. Dana kept pace with ease, while Grampa Banks hung back, a little shamefaced.

"Sorry for dropping you in it there, old man," he said, quietly. "I won't let you down like that again. Ought to have dealt with the blighter meself. Karate chop!"

"I am most glad that you did not 'karate chop' anyone, *mein ami*," replied Bonnie. The only chops Grampa Banks knew anything about were served with apple sauce.

"It's a pity I didn't have my foil," chipped in Dana. "That would have been *quite* a different story."

Bonnie was pretty sure that a foil must be something to do with fencing. But she could not help imagining Dana wrapping Ribble up in kitchen foil and popping him in the oven for forty minutes.

"What're you maunging about, back there?" asked Reuben Ribble, voice raised over the wind.

"My assistants were wondering where you are leading us," lied Bonnie.

"I'm taking you to see *her*." Ribble looked at his watch, then squinted towards the sun. "She should be there about now. I want her to explain to you that I didn't kill anyone. You snitch types never believe folk like me."

"I am not being a *snitch type*," corrected Bonnie, "I am being a private detective."

Reuben Ribble looked back over his shoulder and grunted. "You don't believe me, though, do you?"

Bonnie was not sure what she believed.

"Oh, and it's not a fruit," said Ribble, striding onwards.

"*Pardonnez-me?*" asked Bonnie.

"You said 'forbidden fruit'. An onion is not a *fruit*," said Ribble very slowly, as if he were speaking to a child. (Which he were.) "It's a bulb."

Grampa Banks avoided Bonnie's gaze. She looked to Dana for support.

"He's right," Dana said, apologetically. "I almost said something at the time, but I thought he might be about to murder us."

Bonnie stuffed her hands in her raincoat pockets sulkily and they walked on in silence.

This is why they call detectives 'flatfoots', Bonnie reflected. All this tramping from clue to clue. She hoped the solution to the mystery would be worth the blisters. At least she had not brought her mother on the case. Liz Montgomery had spent the previous month talking about her new step-counter gadget. Three days on the knobbly tracks of Odde Island would have worn it out.

A pleasant little road would have taken them directly across the island, past the thorny hill Bonnie had seen in the centre, but Reuben Ribble had to stop off at the lighthouse to wind up the mechanism. It was a significant detour.

They traipsed on and on and eventually came to the cliffs on Odde Island's far side. There, Bonnie saw a ruined stone tower looking out to sea. The crumbling whitewashed walls were barely taller than Bonnie herself. Still, she could make out where a door and windows had once been.

"A Martello tower, I believe," said Grampa Banks. "Early nineteenth century. Abandoned."

Bonnie could not have guessed how wrong Grampa Banks was.

Reuben Ribble stopped outside the tower's tumbledown doorway and turned.

"Put your fingers in your ears."

Dana and Grampa Banks looked at Bonnie. Bonnie did nothing. Was Reuben Ribble toying with her?

"You aren't members," said Ribble, firmly. "I can't let you hear the password."

Bonnie slowly squeezed her fingers into her ears, eyeing Ribble sceptically. Grampa Banks and Dana followed suit.

The assistant lighthouse keeper glanced around furtively, making sure they were alone, and then swept aside a brush of long grass, revealing a gnarly metal trumpet protruding from the wall. He knocked on the trumpet three times with his medallion.

Tlong! Tlong! Tlong! is the sound Bonnie imagined it made.

She could not resist. She wiggled a finger ever-so-slightly out of her ear, just in time to hear a tinny voice coming from the trumpet say, "Speak softly, friend. What's the password?"

Reuben Ribble lowered his lips to the trumpet and spoke a single word, deadly serious.

"*Onions!*"

And suddenly, the earth seemed to tremble.

A sound like the rattling of chains came from underfoot, accompanied by a groaning, like a shipwreck being hauled up from the seabed. In the centre of the ruined tower, a great iron trapdoor creaked open, like the rusty mouth of a buried giant.

Reuben Ribble gestured for Bonnie to remove her fingers from her ears, and spoke with pride in his gruff voice.

"Welcome ... to the Speak Softly Shop."

With a hand on the trapdoor, he stepped down into the hole and began to descend on a worn wooden staircase. Bonnie watched him *clomp, clomp, clomp* into the shadows.

"Well, hurry up," he called back, softly, before vanishing completely.

"What an absolutely beezer spot for a smuggler's den," said Dana, breathlessly.

Dana was right: a hidden trapdoor in the centre of a circle of white stone was a fitting place for the onion ring to meet. You might even call it *beezer*.

"I should probably go first," said Grampa Banks, eyeing the gloomy steps. "Could be a trap?"

"*Non, mein ami.* Montgomery Bonbon, he is always the first to get to the bottom of a mystery," said Bonnie, showing a little more confidence than she felt.

With her assistants in tow, Bonnie climbed down, down, down a long, low-ceilinged tunnel. She had expected the sour scents of damp earth and wet rock, but the deeper she travelled, the more inviting the tunnel smelled.

"Mind out for the broken step," Reuben Ribble warned, just in time for Bonnie to hop over it. "We have to guard against non-members."

Sometimes Bonnie thought the tunnel was natural, formed over an unthinkably long span of time by wind and waves. Other times, she thought she saw marks where ancient tools had carved a pathway through the rock.

"This is incredible, Monsieur," said Dana, wide-eyed. "Much older than the ruined tower, I'd wager. Mother would love this place!"

"Your mother is not a member," said their guide, sternly. "I'm only letting you folks in so Mr Detective here can see the truth: Reuben Ribble is no murderer."

Without warning, the narrow tunnel opened out and Bonnie found herself standing in a vast, shimmering cave. Warm, orange lights made the interior feel like a candlelit banqueting hall.

Glistening stalactites hung down like melted wax above people seated at makeshift tables constructed from barrels and driftwood.

"Look!" breathed Dana.

"Onions!" said Grampa Banks.

In one alcove, Bonnie could see huge bowls of onion stew steaming away irresistibly. In another nook, revellers dipped hunks of bread into an onion soup fountain. Elsewhere, great vats simmered, onion bhajis bubbled and chopped onions caramelized. Onion rings were rung; spring onions were sprung!

Bonnie took a deep breath. The smell was incredible. Both her eyes and her mouth were watering.

Click, FLASH, grrr...

At the flash of Grampa Banks's camera, the denizens of the smugglers' hideout stopped shovelling onions into their mouths. They gawped at Montgomery Bonbon and his entourage as they passed through the cave of oniony wonders. Bonnie was

looking for Reuben Ribble's accomplice: Miss Bunch.

"Ah, Monsieur Bonbon. Welcome to the Speak Softly Shop," came the voice of a woman, emerging from coiling tendrils of onion-steam. "Are you here to shut us down, or shall I do you a nice shallot?"

Bonnie rubbed her bleary eyes and blinked again. The speaker was not Miss Bunch.

"We had a good run, eh, Ribble?" said the woman, cracking her knobbly knuckles. "Will you be clapping us in irons now, Detective?

"L-Lady Wallop?" Bonnie stumbled. "You are being the smuggler's accomplice?!"

Lady Wallop bit into a slice of onion quiche and chewed slowly, frowning curiously. "You were expecting someone else?"

"*Non, non*," Bonnie lied.

"But you said—" began Dana, before Bonnie silenced her with a sharp twitch of the moustache.

"Is that Rita Hornville's girl?" asked Lady Wallop. "Looking to become a member?"

"I am assisting Monsieur Bonbon in investigating the suspicious deaths of Maude Cragge and Tobias

Waterman," said Dana with obvious satisfaction.

"Can I interest you in an onion fritter? Perhaps a mug of onion beer for Mr Banks?"

"No thank you. I'm driving," replied Grampa Banks, presumably because it was more polite than going, "Yuck!"

"Then what, pray, can I do for you?" asked Lady Wallop.

"You can tell the truth," said Bonnie with a dramatic flourish of her index finger.

"The little one with the 'tashe reckons I did Maude Cragge in," explained Reuben Ribble flatly.

Lady Wallop rolled her eyes.

"All right, Monsieur, I admit it. Mr Ribble and I are smugglers," she said, leaning in close. "Smugglers, yes. *Murderers*, absolutely not. Now, I shouldn't have lied to you about what we got up to on the night of the storm. But you must see why I couldn't tell you the whole story?"

"When you lie to Bonbon, you strike the blow against justice herself," declared Bonnie with as much severity as she could muster. "Now, the truth, if you please. What exactly were you doing on the night Maude Cragge died?"

Lady Wallop sighed. "As I'm sure you've deduced, I was driving a shipment of contraband onions across the island in my camper van. Ribble landed his rowing boat on Peeble Beach. I picked him up and we drove here – *directly*. Good thing too, otherwise we never would have got the goods back before the rain started. I do loathe that wet onion smell."

"So you see, I *did* go to the mainland," said Reuben Ribble smugly. "I just didn't *drive*. And I didn't go anywhere near the lighthouse all night."

"Quite," added Lady Wallop. "We stayed down here until dawn, and a dozen people in this cave will swear to that."

Lady Wallop nibbled her onion quiche down to the crust. "So," she said, "you can dob us in and spoil everyone's supper – OR you can take my word for it that Ribble and I are merely innocent smugglers." Lady Wallop laid a hand on her heart and set her jaw firmly. "And a Wallop's word is worth a lot of onions round these parts."

"Do you swear to it also, Monsieur Ribble?" asked Bonnie.

He nodded. "Smuggler's honour."

"*Bon*," said Bonnie at last.

"Now, you'd better skedaddle and catch the *real* killer. But before you go," said Lady Wallop, clapping her hands together, "let's have some onion rings for our guests!"

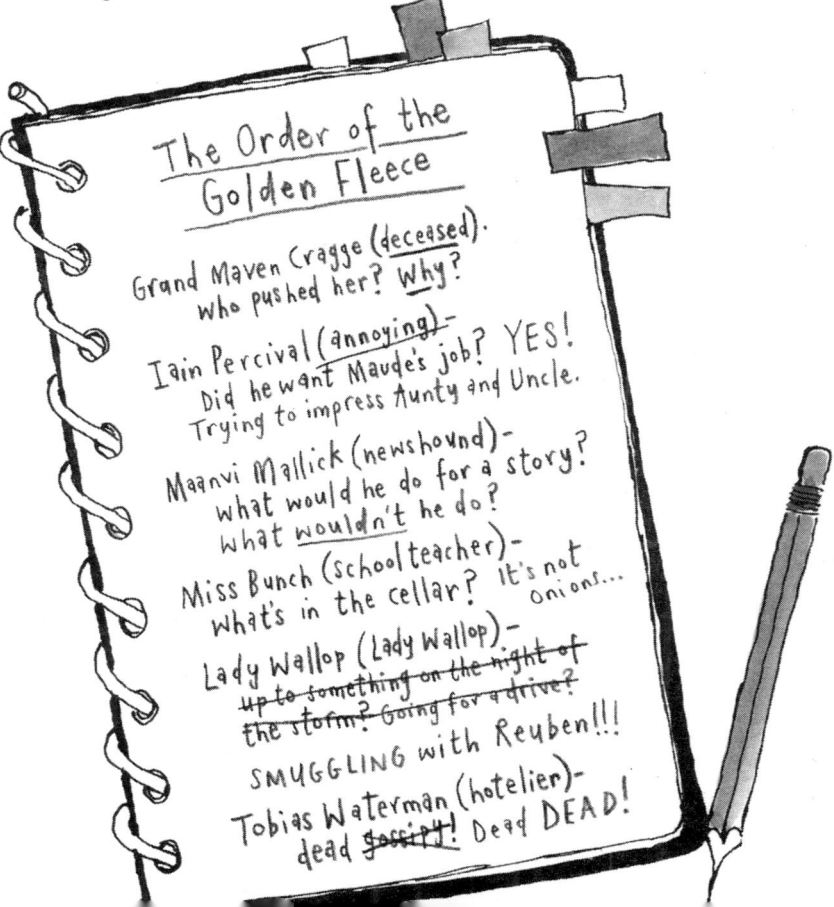

The Order of the Golden Fleece

Grand Maven Cragge (deceased).
Who pushed her? Why?

Iain Percival (annoying) —
Did he want Maude's job? YES!
Trying to impress Aunty and Uncle.

Maanvi Mallick (newshound) —
What would he do for a story?
What wouldn't he do?

Miss Bunch (schoolteacher) —
What's in the cellar? It's not onions...

Lady Wallop (Lady Wallop) —
~~up to something on the night of the storm? Going for a drive?~~
SMUGGLING with Reuben!!!

Tobias Waterman (hotelier) —
dead ~~gossip!~~ Dead DEAD!

Chapter Fifteen
Oddefellas

The cloud hanging over the local Oddities had only grown stormier with the death of Tobias Waterman. But despite worried faces, the harbour was still abustle with preparations for the pageant. Garlands were hung from lamp posts, bobble hats were placed on postboxes and rubber ducks were glued to statues. Odde Harbour marked the starting point of the parade – and the attitude of the locals seemed to be that *the pageant must go on*.

The journey back had given Bonnie a chance to wring half a pint of sweet onion grease out of her moustache. She took some satisfaction in having busted the smugglers, but what had promised to be a solid lead in Bonnie's case had turned out to be a wild goose chase. And nobody wanted to chase a wild goose. Except, perhaps, another goose with a thing for bad boys.

Every good detective knows about the Doldrums. They are where you end up when a case has you stumped. When all your leads have taken you down dead ends, that is when the Doldrums creep up on you and whisper, *"It's impossible ... Give up."*

Bonnie was not ready to let that happen just yet. So, Miss Bunch was *not* the brains behind the onion ring. Then what on earth was she hiding in the schoolhouse cellar? Bonnie could hardly imagine a secret so terrible that the sweet schoolteacher could be driven to murder to protect it. But she had to know – what was down there?

The schoolhouse was empty when Bessie trundled past, the sloping cellar door still fastened with a heavy padlock. There was only one person on the island who could pass through a locked door, and it was not Montgomery Bonbon. Eventually they tracked their latest suspect down to a quaint little ice-cream parlour named Oddefellas: the kind of place where you could order dishes that no one had ever heard of before.

It was Dana who spotted Miss Bunch.

"Is that her? Flowery hat at three o'clock!" Dana whispered.

Never mind three o'clock – Miss Bunch's obviously home-made hat was flowery all day long. Under a striped awning, they saw the teacher devouring a scoop of pistachio and elderflower ice cream, served in a baby's shoe.

"And look there, it's that awful newsletter chap," said Grampa Banks.

He was right. Two tables over from Miss Bunch sat Maanvi Mallick. He was enjoying a blob of rosehip and coriander sorbet served in a flowerpot. Well, he was eating it – there was no evidence he was enjoying it. Mallick's presence made things more complicated. Bonnie could hardly interrogate Miss Bunch under the watchful eyes of the *Odde Argus*.

"The situation," she warned Grampa Banks and Dana, "it is like the paper flowers upon the hat of Fräulein Bunch. It must be handled most delicately. Please to follow my lead."

Bonnie checked her moustache, positioned her beret at a jaunty angle and set off across the cobbles towards Oddefellas. She remembered Maanvi Mallick's tendency to keep glancing over her shoulder when he spoke to her. The crafty newshound was always on the lookout for fresh dirt to dig. If Bonnie wanted to get rid of him now, she needed to throw the dog a bone.

Bonnie entered the ice-cream parlour and nodded a greeting towards the reporter, who brightened up.

"Well, if it isn't the tireless gumshoe himself!" Maanvi Mallick smiled, devouring another spoonful of sorbet. "How goes the case? Collared any crooks I should know about?"

Bonnie did not answer. Instead, she selected a table between Maanvi Mallick and Miss Bunch, and sent Grampa Banks up to the counter. He purchased a hibiscus wafer in the shape of an oyster – much against his will.

"I sold ice cream for thirty-odd years," Grampa Banks grumbled as he returned to their table. "No one ever said, 'Got any hibiscus, mate? And can I have it in a shoe?'"

"*Tranquil, mein ami,*" soothed Bonnie. Her grandfather was as serious about ice cream as she was about fighting crime. He once sold ice cream on Widdlington Pier during a hailstorm. The winds were

so high, a Strawberry Ice Plop was blown all the way to Brussels, where it landed on a man's head and foiled a bank robbery. Maanvi Mallick would have loved that story.

Brave Bloke Busts Belgian Bank Baddie!

"And who do I see here?" asked Mallick with a smirk, jabbing his spoon towards Dana. "Don't tell me the precocious young Hornville is in the frame for murder?"

Dana scowled at him. Suddenly the ice cream was no longer the coldest thing in the room.

"Speaking of acquired tastes, have you tried the sorbet?" Mallick laughed. "One out of five stars from the *Odde Argus*, but hey – Maanvi Mallick never misses a scoop!"

Nothing, not even the total silence that followed his joke, seemed to put him off.

"But suspicious deaths make for even better copy than bad reviews. A newsman's gotta dig dirt, you know? So, on the level now, Bonbon. Can I get a few words for my readers?"

Bonnie could think of a few words she would like to say to the reporter. Words such as *bog off* and *mind your own business*. But she had to be more subtle than that.

"*Natürlich,*" she said carefully, "Montgomery Bonbon, he would be delighted to speak – how do you say? – on the record."

If Maanvi Mallick had leaned any closer, he would have fallen off his chair.

"Provided that you agree to keep – how do you say? – *hush-hush* about ... the treasure."

The only sound in Oddefellas was Maanvi Mallick's spoon dropping into his flowerpot.

"T-treasure?" he asked.

"Treasure?" asked Dana and Grampa Banks in harmony.

Maanvi Mallick fumbled a notepad out of his pocket.

Bonnie had been thinking on her feet, and those feet were very tired from crossing a distinctly lumpsome island. She had tried to conjure up something that would interest Mallick more than her investigation. And, well, treasure and islands went together like ice cream and ... a baby's shoe.

"*Ja*, the treasure," repeated Bonnie, trying to wink at both Grampa Banks and Dana at the same time. It came out as a blink.

Dana caught on quickly. "The treasure, of course!" she said, tapping her nose. "Mum's the word."

Grampa Banks looked a little discombobulated, although that might have been caused by the olive on his hibiscus ice cream.

"Oh, the *treasure*!" he chimed in eventually.

"Yes, best to keep it hush-hush. Don't want the general public getting wind of it, eh, old man?"

Bonnie pretended not to notice Maanvi Mallick's pencil scribbling away furiously.

"Mother thinks it might be Viking," lied Dana. "Or even Roman."

"Or even ... *Egyptian!*" added Grampa Banks.

If Grampa Banks was going too far, Maanvi Mallick had not noticed. His pencil was moving so fast Bonnie half expected to see smoke rising from the paper. She knew she had to cut in before Grampa Banks added the Crown Jewels and the Great Wall of China to their fictitious treasure trove.

"*Ja, ja,*" she said casually. "And this find most extraordinary has been buried for a thousand years at the top of that thorny hill."

The reporter was squeezing his pencil tightly enough to snap it in two.

"Hill? You mean Hillikin Knowe? The one in the middle of the island?" demanded Mallick.

The hill was a perfectly good spot for an imaginary treasure to be buried, Bonnie thought.

And it was a long, long way from Oddefellas.

She nodded. "*Ja.*"

"Blimey! It'll be swarming with pageant-goers tomorrow," said Maanvi Mallick, grabbing his overcoat. "I'd better act fast!"

With a sound like a pigeon taking flight, the reporter disappeared through the ice-cream parlour door, leaving his spoon spinning in an empty flowerpot.

Bonnie winked at Dana and Grampa Banks, one at a time. "A newsman must – how do you say? – dig the dirt," she said slyly.

Dana laughed at the silly trick they had played on the reporter, and even Bonnie felt a small smile curl underneath her moustache.

Grampa Banks was not quite so amused. "I suppose I'll have to pay his bill now," he grumbled.

Miss Bunch had been watching the proceedings. She clapped her hands together in a delicate round of applause. "Masterful! Quite masterful, Monsieur."

"Ah! Fräulein Bunch," said Bonnie, acting as if she had only just noticed the schoolteacher.

"Hush now, Monsieur," said Miss Bunch with a smile. "Fingers on lips. You knew very well I was here. And, if it's finally my turn to be hauled over the coals, I must warn you..." She glanced down at her ice cream and winced. "I may just have eaten a shoelace."

Interrogating Miss Bunch felt like trampling on a patch of daisies. But Bonnie had no choice if she wanted answers. She steepled her fingers and gave a single sharp twitch of her moustache.

"Please to tell us what you are hiding in the schoolhouse cellar that you were so keen to keep from the sight of Bonbon?"

Miss Bunch paused. Then, unexpectedly, she laughed.

It was a chortling, warbling kind of laughter, like water bubbling out of a natural spring, like a basketful of butterflies being released and fluttering off in every direction, like a ticklish piano going through a car wash.

"Oh, Monsieur!" she said eventually. "I wanted it to be a surprise. But I suppose you'll see them tomorrow anyway. Come along with me to the schoolhouse, and I'll show you."

Chapter Sixteen
The Schoolhouse Cellar

As a general rule, if a cellar is home to a scene of bloodcurdling terror, the staircase leading down to it ought to be rotten and draped in cobwebs. The staircase beneath the schoolhouse was instead made of sturdy pine. The wood did not even creak like cellar steps are supposed to. Compared with the tunnel leading down to the smugglers' hideout, it was positively cosy.

There was nothing to prepare Bonnie for the sight that awaited her.

Miss Bunch had gone first, disappearing into the darkness. Making sure that Dana and Grampa Banks were close behind her, Bonnie followed the schoolteacher through the sloping door and down the steps into the cellar.

"Light switch ... light switch..." Miss Bunch sang to herself. "There we go! Everybody in?"

With a fizzing sound, a single light bulb flickered on and shone weakly in the gloom. Looking around, Bonnie saw old school desks and chairs, a stack of paint tins and ... something else. In the furthest depths of the cellar, she saw weird, lumpen shadows.

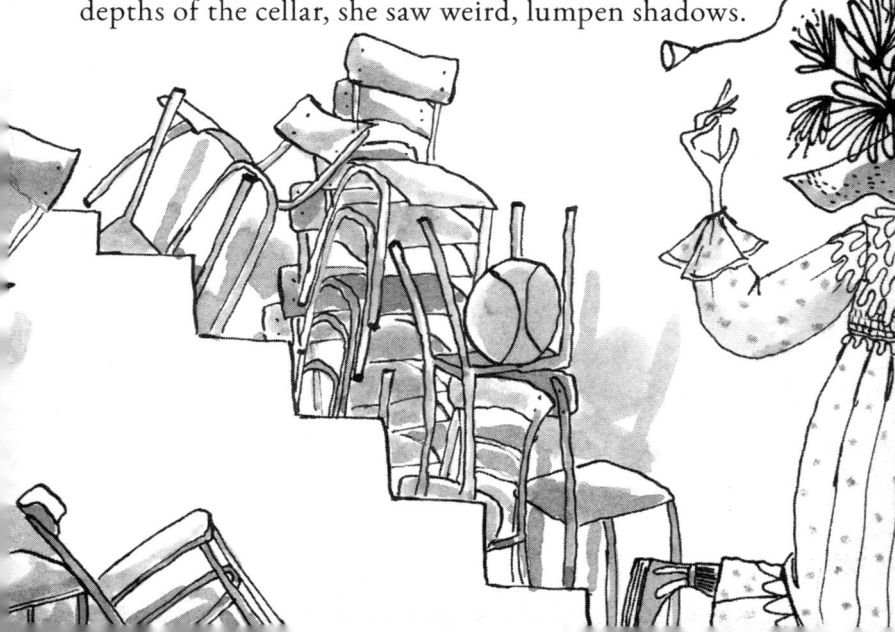

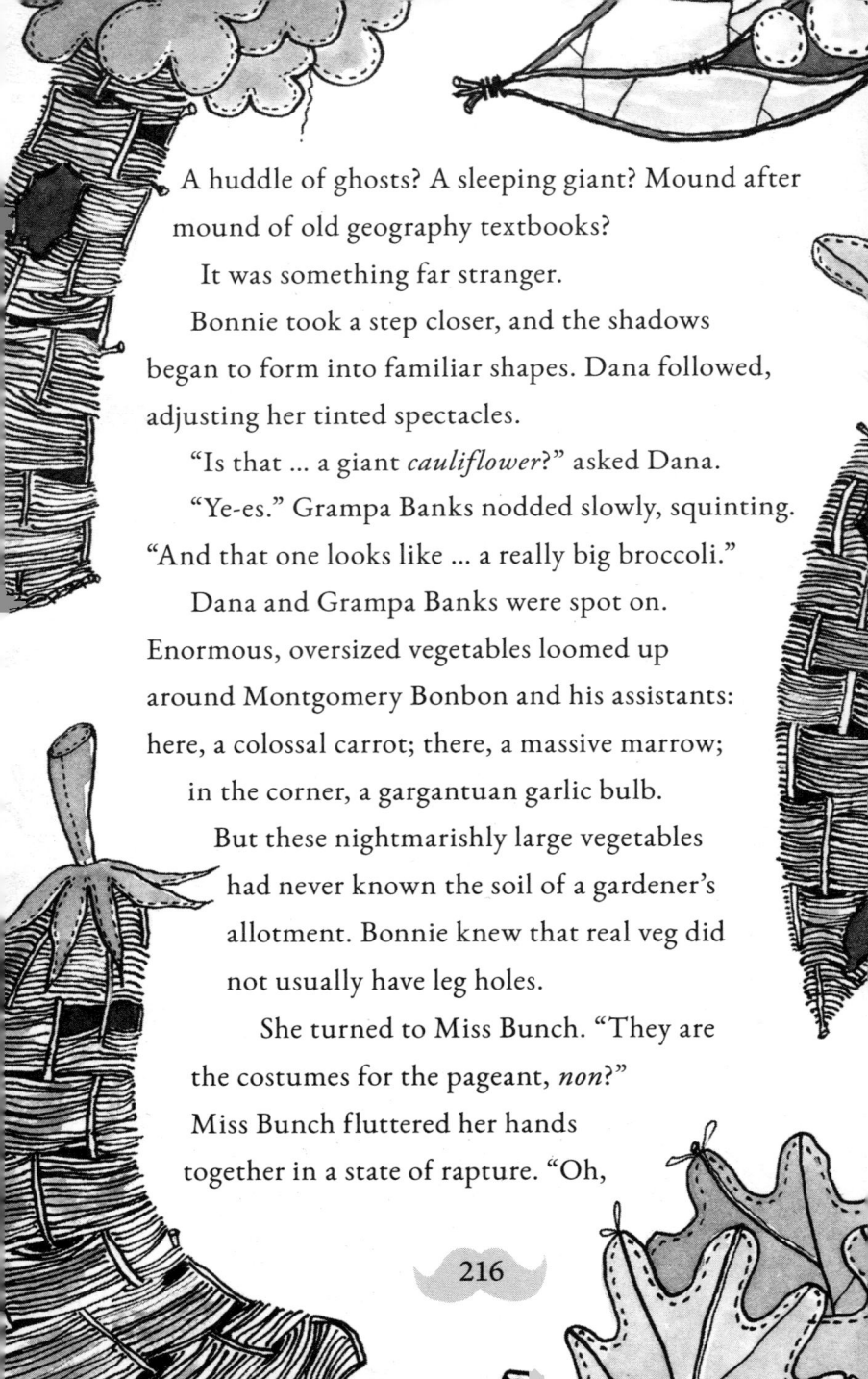

A huddle of ghosts? A sleeping giant? Mound after mound of old geography textbooks?

It was something far stranger.

Bonnie took a step closer, and the shadows began to form into familiar shapes. Dana followed, adjusting her tinted spectacles.

"Is that ... a giant *cauliflower*?" asked Dana.

"Ye-es." Grampa Banks nodded slowly, squinting. "And that one looks like ... a really big broccoli."

Dana and Grampa Banks were spot on. Enormous, oversized vegetables loomed up around Montgomery Bonbon and his assistants: here, a colossal carrot; there, a massive marrow; in the corner, a gargantuan garlic bulb.

But these nightmarishly large vegetables had never known the soil of a gardener's allotment. Bonnie knew that real veg did not usually have leg holes.

She turned to Miss Bunch. "They are the costumes for the pageant, *non*?"

Miss Bunch fluttered her hands together in a state of rapture. "Oh,

I'm so glad you appreciate them, Monsieur. I've been working on these designs all year."

Bonnie remembered now that Miss Bunch made her own *unique* dresses. But the costumes were something else altogether.

Bonnie laid a hand on the rough surface of a supersized savoy cabbage; Dana grappled with a mammoth mushroom; Grampa Banks popped his head inside a Brobdingnagian beetroot. He wriggled one of his arms out through an armhole (or a mouthhole?) and waved at Bonnie.

"M've mver seen the like!" he said, muffled by Miss Bunch's savoury creation.

"It's not a hobby for me, it's a *calling*. More than a lifetime's work," continued Miss Bunch solemnly. "A Bunch has *always* designed the costumes for the Odde Island Pageant. It's tradition."

Bonnie could see that the outsized outfits were constructed from woven willow stems and papier mâché, and decorated with colourful silks and sequins. Close up, they were even more misshapen and grotesque than they had first seemed.

"Most lifelike, Fräulein," said Bonnie, quite dishonestly.

Miss Bunch swelled with pride and skipped over towards Bonnie.

"Sometimes I try them on in the schoolyard. I do it at night, you understand, because I don't want anyone seeing the costumes. Ah – no pictures before the big day, please, Mr Banks! If you keep playing with that camera, I'll put it in my desk drawer and you'll get it back at home time."

Grampa Banks took his finger off the shutter button and murmured something that sounded like a very tiny "Sorry, Miss."

"I had been test-driving a pumpkin when you came by the other night," Miss Bunch continued. "I do hope I didn't look *too* suspicious!"

Bonnie curled her moustache thoughtfully. It had seemed pretty fishy at the time, but there was nothing particularly fishy about a cellar full of pageant costumes. In fact, there was nothing fishy about Miss Bunch's designs at all. Although there was something a little off about the pumpkin.

Eyebrows raised, Grampa Banks whispered, "Has that pumpkin got a..."

"...posterior?" finished Dana quietly.

All of Miss Bunch's costumes were covered in unsightly lumps and bumps – Bonnie was sure this could not be intentional. But, somehow, the schoolteacher had managed to craft a pumpkin outfit with a very distinct and very round bottom.

There was no delicate way of putting it: it was a pumpkin with a bum.

It was a bumkin.

Bonnie had to chew her moustache to keep from laughing. She could hear Dana snorting and Grampa Banks's distinctive wheeze. She attempted to carry on without making eye contact with her assistants.

"What a ... fine ... fine piece," Bonnie managed at last, her moustache quivering at the thought of the poor fools who would have to parade around the island in these ridiculous, itchy-looking monstrosities.

"Oh, Monsieuuuuur!" trilled Miss Bunch, clasping her hands together in anticipation. "I'm so pleased you like it, because I've been meaning to ask.

There's one very special costume I've been working on, and, well..."

Oh no. Bonnie's heart sank. Her stomach lurched. Her other organs were not best pleased.

"I think it would suit you down to the ground!"

Bonnie's beret, moustache and raincoat were neatly bundled away in her yellow backpack, and she sat at a table outside Oddefellas with Dana and Grampa Banks. Dana had persuaded the staff to make a pot of mint tea to help revive Bonnie. They had served it in a jam jar with a candy cane.

"What exactly did I just agree to?" Bonnie asked slowly.

Dana grinned. "*You* didn't agree to anything, but Montgomery Bonbon said he would be *the most delighted* to play the onion in the Odde Island Pageant."

Bonnie groaned. That was why Miss Bunch had been doodling onions. She had been working on a costume design.

"Miss Bunch was over the moon to have a *celebrity* wear one of her" – Dana searched for the right word – "creations."

"But I don't *want* to be an onion!" protested Bonnie.

It was Grampa Banks's turn to grin. "It could be worse. If they put you in that pumpkin, you'd be … Montgomery Bumbum!"

He and Dana fell about giggling. Bonnie, however, did not feel like laughing right now.

"I'm sorry, love. You see, apparently the pageant commemorates the … um … outlawing of onions on the island," explained Grampa Banks. "The whole thing is very … what do you call it?"

"Symbolic," said Dana.

"It's very *symbolic*, yes. The onion costume represents…" Grampa Banks thought for a moment. The girls watched him closely.

"Onions," he concluded.

Bonnie slumped in her chair. Dana's mother was right: the practices of the people on Odde Island really were unique.

"Look, forget about all that," said Dana, dropping her voice to an excited whisper. She tapped that morning's edition of the *Odde Argus*. A sub-headline read: *Send For Sands!*

"That inspector from the mainland will be here in the morning. Have we solved the case yet? Who pushed Maude Cragge? Who killed Tobias Waterman? How did the killer escape from Waterman's locked office?"

The afternoon was clear, but Bonnie felt like a thick sea fog had rolled in. She had been so certain that she was getting closer and closer to unravelling the mysteries of Odde Island, but now the answers which had begun to seem so near were vanishing into the mist. The schoolhouse cellar had turned out to be *another* dead end, just like the smugglers' hideout.

"Let me have another look at those notes we made," said Bonnie, playing for time.

Dana rummaged around in Bonnie's backpack while Grampa Banks pushed aside her jam jar to make space. Dana unfolded the papers and maps and spread them across the table. Grampa Banks added freshly developed snaps of the crime scenes. The clues were almost tumbling off the edges of the little table. None of them seemed to fit together.

"So how does this normally work, Mr Banks?" Dana asked. "Does Bonnie snap her fingers and say 'Huzzah!' when she cracks it?"

"No," said Grampa Banks diplomatically, "she never says 'Huzzah!', exactly. But she does have her Eureka Moments, oh yes."

"Eureka Moments," said Dana, relishing the words. "Oh, that's good! *Eureka Moments*," she repeated slowly, as if it were a box of fancy chocolates.

For some reason, it irritated Bonnie to see Dana and Grampa Banks getting along so well. They were supposed to be helping her solve the case, but instead they were just chatting while staring at her expectantly.

"Well, I can't do it if you're looking at me," she protested, folding her arms huffily. "I haven't got Eureka Moments on tap. They happen when they happen."

She could feel the pressure building up inside her middle. That might have been partly to do with the onions rings she had eaten earlier. But she was sure it was mostly to do with the case. It just did not make sense. Bonnie shuffled the notes until she found the timeline she and Dana had drawn up.

> Timeline
> 11pm Tobias spoke to Maude. He was in guest house.
> ? Maude goes to top of lighthouse.
> 11.30pm Started to rain.
> 12am Lighthouse stops. Search party sets out. Miss Bunch, Iain Percival and Maarin Mallick meet in the harbour.

"OK, OK. According to the timeline, Maude Cragge died at some point between Tobias Waterman's phone call to the lighthouse at eleven and the start of the rain half an hour later," she began.

Grampa Banks and Dana nodded in perfect synchronicity.

"We know the lighthouse lantern stopped turning

at midnight. Iain Percival and Miss Bunch went to investigate, along with Maanvi Mallick. We've worked out it takes well over an hour to get from the lighthouse to Odde Harbour on foot. Even with wheels, you can't do it in less than an hour. So that means none of them could have killed Maude Cragge and got back in time to set off again. All three of them have alibis."

Grampa Banks and Dana nodded together. "Alibis."

"And Lady Wallop and Reuben Ribble were onion smuggling, so they have alibis too, yes?"

"Yes," agreed Grampa Banks and Dana.

"And then Tobias Waterman was struck dead with an antique blunderbuss in a sealed room."

Bonnie picked up a wafer biscuit and dropped it into her empty jam jar.

"And the room was locked from the inside," she said, clamping one hand over the top of the jar.

"Locked," said Dana.

"From the inside," said Grampa Banks.

Bonnie tapped the jam jar with a fingernail. The wafer biscuit inside did absolutely nothing. It lay utterly still, just like Tobias Waterman had done when Bonnie found him.

"So, there you have it," said Bonnie, pushing the jam jar away and standing up. "Both murders are completely impossible. Let's go back to Widdlington before I have to dress up like an onion."

"Oh, come on, love. You can't give up; you're just in the Doldrums."

"Please," begged Dana, "this is my first murder case. We have to solve it."

Bonnie found herself walking in an angry little circle around their table.

"You're not listening!" she said a little bit too loudly. "It's just the facts. And the facts don't make sense."

She slapped the pile of papers in frustration. Her fingers were sticky from the candy cane, and her hand came away with a copy of the *Odde Argus*.

"The facts..." Bonnie repeated.

What was it Maanvi Mallick had said when they first met? He had told Montgomery Bonbon that the *Odde Argus* printed the facts, and a little bit extra.

"Flamin' Nora!" cried Bonnie, slapping her other hand to her forehead.

"Eureka Moment?" asked Dana hopefully.

"Flamin' Nora Moment," corrected Grampa Banks.

"The facts don't make sense," said Bonnie again, smoothing the wrinkly newsletter out on the table, "so someone has to be lying. All along we've been assuming that the report in the *Odde Argus* is correct. What if it isn't? Mallick could have lied about the timings to cover up doing the deed himself!"

"You don't mean..." said Dana. "He wouldn't have bumped off Maude Cragge just to have a good story to write, would he?"

"I wouldn't put anything past that one," said Grampa Banks grimly. "He's got more cheek than a bumkin."

Bonnie's sea fog had not quite cleared, but she thought she could see a light up ahead. Was it leading the HMS *Bonbon* to safe harbour, or to be dashed on the rocks? There was only one way to be sure.

"I think it's time we dug some dirt on Maanvi Mallick himself," announced Bonnie. "And I think I've got a plan."

"Bravo!" cheered Grampa Banks.

"Huzzah!" cried Dana, snapping her fingers.

Bonnie placed a hand on her friend's shoulder. "Dana," she said with a sly grin, "how do you feel about dressing up as a massive onion?"

The Odde Argus

TRAGEDY AT LEERIE LIGHTHOUSE!

BY MAANVI MALLICK, NEWSHOUND

GRAND MAVEN IN DEATH PLUNGE

Odde Island is in shock, after high winds claimed the life of lighthouse keeper Maude Cragge.

The alarm was raised at midnight by exciseman Iain Percival, when he noticed that our beloved clockwork lighthouse lantern had stopped turning. This reporter braved lashing rain and soggy sandals to join Mr Percival and schoolteacher Miss Bunch on a perilous trek from Odde Harbour across the storm-battered island.

CRAGGE'S BODY FOUND

Reaching Solan Cliffs well after 1 a Ms Cragge's body was discovered a foot of the lighthouse. It is bel that the unfortunate keeper had

Orion Costume by Miss Bunch

Chapter Seventeen
The Plan

Bonnie Montgomery had never seen a seaplane before. The name made it sound like a vehicle from a daydream, like a cloud car or a space kayak.

But the appearance of the seaplane itself was far less fantastical. Looking like a small aeroplane wearing an enormous pair of clogs, it sploshed down onto the waters of Odde Harbour, bouncing and bobbing in the foam like a clumsy duckling.

Inspector Sands had chosen to arrive in the most unnecessarily ostentatious way possible. If she had waited a few hours, she could have driven across the causeway without any fuss. But, Bonnie knew, the inspector liked to make a splash.

It was still early on the day of the Odde Island Pageant, and the morning air seemed to hum with a sense of anticipation. The houses were festooned with flowers and decorated with paper lanterns. Colourful bunting had been bunted all across the harbour, but a shadow hung over the festivities. The people gathered on the harbourside were buzzing not because of the upcoming parade, but because of the impending arrival of Inspector Sands of Widdlington Constabulary.

The crowd was mostly made up of onlookers – with a few bystanders here and there – alongside Bonnie Montgomery, Grampa Banks and two members of the Order of the Golden Fleece.

Squinting in the low morning sun, they watched Roz Baillie row out in a small boat to meet the inspector. The especial constable did not look especially confident on the water. And it cannot have helped that Inspector Sands was hanging out of the seaplane shouting things like "Heave-ho!", "Pull!" and "The oars, woman! Use the oars!"

The constable's little jolly-boat became a lot less jolly the moment Inspector Sands set foot in it. She insisted on waving to her harbourside audience as Roz started to row back, causing the boat to wobble wildly. They came close to capsizing more than once before Inspector Sands's shiny boots finally landed on Odde Island. Roz gave her a boost out of the boat, and then clambered out herself.

"Welcome ... to Odde Island ... ma'am," she gasped, drenched in sweat. "Especial Constable ... Roz Baillie. Your reputation ... precedes you. But ... I never knew ... you could fly a seaplane."

"Neither did I," said the inspector briskly, scanning the harbour with a critical eye. "But it's like riding a thingumabob, isn't it? You pick it up as you go along."

Bonnie did not know how to fly a seaplane either. But she found herself wondering if the propellers were still supposed to be spinning after you had got off. And whether or not one wing was meant to be underwater. She sighed as bubbles escaped from the sinking plane and the current began to slowly pull it under. Sending Inspector Sands to solve a mystery was like sending a bull to do your china shopping.

With a great deal of jostling and the sound of elbows being poked into ribs, Iain Percival and Maanvi Mallick emerged from the crowd and began speaking loudly and at the same time.

"Inspector! Can you comment on rumours that the recent deaths are connected to the treasure—"

"ON behalf of the Odde Island Order of the Golden Fleece, permit me, IN my capacity as spokesperson—"

"—and my readers are asking, will Montgomery Bonbon stay on the case?"

"—to welcome you to the island IN your capacity as police inspector—"

"Oh, that's quite enough of that," interrupted Inspector Sands.

She snatched Maanvi Mallick's notepad with one hand and Iain Percival's clipboard with the other, and frisbeed them both into the harbour.

"I'm in charge now," she announced, eyeing the bugle Iain Percival was holding behind his back. "And if you make even a sound with that oojamaflip, I'll stick a cork in it so hard you'll blow your own ears off. Understood?"

Iain Percival nodded glumly, and slunk away into the crowd, while Maanvi Mallick adjusted his hat and produced a fresh notebook from somewhere about his person.

"So, where is he?" demanded Inspector Sands, stretching her calves absent-mindedly.

"Where's who, ma'am?" asked Roz Baillie, looking a little peaky.

"Bonbon, of course, the amateur whatsisname. Just like him to try and muscle in on a good murder."

Grampa Banks stepped forward and cleared his throat loudly. "Perhaps I can help, Inspector. Clive Banks, we've met before."

"Oh, aye? Banks, is it? You're Bonbon's whatchamacallit, aren't you?"

"I suppose I am," replied Grampa Banks in far too polite a tone. "I don't think you've met my granddaughter."

"Good morning, Inspector," said Bonnie with a big fake smile. She was not wearing the moustache. She was not wearing the raincoat. And she was being seen by Inspector Sands.

This was all part of the plan.

"You anyone important, are you?" asked Inspector Sands brusquely.

"Definitely not," replied Bonnie meekly.

"Well, stop wasting police time then. It's a crime, you know. I could have you arrested. Now, where is that interfering little fella with the stupid 'tache?"

"He's over there," said Bonnie, pointing at a little square on the far side of the harbour, where locals were preparing flaming torches and barrels for the day's festivities.

This time, it was Inspector Sands's turn to look sickly. She grabbed Roz Baillie and twisted the poor especial constable's head towards the square.

"Tell me, lass ... what do you see over there?"

Roz swallowed loudly. "It looks like a lot of giant vegetables, ma'am. Doing a dance, ma'am."

"Thank whatsisname for that!" said the inspector, slapping Roz on the back. "For a moment there, I thought I was having a turn."

Indeed, on the far side of the harbour, Miss Bunch was leading several unfortunates in a rehearsal of the day's revelries. Most of them were dressed in the giant vegetable costumes, and at the head was a large round white onion.

"That you over there, Bonbon?" yelled the inspector in an even louder voice than usual.

In the middle of the square, the onion broke off from the incomprehensible dance and waved over at the crowd.

Inspector Sands tutted. "There's no telling what these wannabe detectives will get themselves into. Especially the foreign ones, mark you. Still, with Bonbon out of the way, I might get a chance to solve this one." She clapped her hands together with satisfaction. "Make way for the police!"

No one was blocking the inspector's way, but the crowd obediently parted even wider to allow her to pass. Roz Baillie scurried after her, shaking seawater from her shirtsleeves.

Bonnie was rather pleased with how well the plan was going. Everyone believed that Montgomery Bonbon was taking a lead role in the Odde Island Pageant, when in fact Dana was the unlucky onion wearer. No one would be able to tell the difference between Dana's impression of Montgomery Bonbon's funny voice and the real thing. Not underneath the muffling layers of onion.

Bonnie could not imagine how hot and unpleasant it was for Dana inside the costume. Or rather, she *could* imagine it, and she was very glad to be wearing her own clothes. The genius of Bonnie's plan was that it enabled her to traverse the island unobserved and it got her out of looking like an absolute plum. Or rather, onion.

She intended to pay a little visit to Maanvi Mallick's home and start digging. Everyone would be watching the celebrations, including the newspaperman. And this was where Grampa Banks came in: he had volunteered to photograph the pageant for the *Odde Argus* – the perfect excuse for him to stick to Mallick like a limpet covered in jam. Pretending not to loathe the reporter would be the biggest challenge of Grampa Banks's crime-solving career to date, but he would do it. Anything for Montgomery Bonbon.

Bonnie was getting closer to the truth. Nothing, she thought, could stop her now.

"Locked!"

Bonnie rattled the handle and cursed and dratted. What was the point of coming to a quaint little island where people could leave their back doors open, if people did not actually leave their back doors open?

Maanvi Mallick's cottage had no cat flap and no conveniently open windows. Bonnie wriggled her fingers in the hope of stimulating blood flow to the problem-solving centre of her brain. If a locked door was no barrier to murder, then it ought to be no barrier to justice.

People often kept a spare key hidden near their door for emergency situations. And solving a murder was certainly an emergency. Bonnie knew that her mum kept a key hidden inside a hollow rock that looked completely out of place in their concrete front yard in Widdlington. But where would Maanvi Mallick conceal a spare?

She surveyed her surroundings. Mallick's home was a whitewashed, one-storey cottage next to the clifftop path. With so little space for a backyard, a jumble of garden paraphernalia had been squeezed in between the cottage and the path: plant pots; beanpoles; a rusty coal scuttle; a boot scraper; a sack of compost with a trowel sticking out; a row of thirsty-looking sunflowers; a garden gnome who was missing his fishing rod; and a welcome mat that said *READ THE ODDE ARGUS!*

Bonnie peeled up all four corners of the welcome mat, much to the annoyance of the woodlice who lived in the damp slice of reality between the mat and the flagstone below. There was no key there. She shuffled plant pots and rattled the coal scuttle.

Not a single key.

Bonnie racked her brain. What did she know about Maanvi Mallick? He was a newspaperman, through and through. That much was certain. He liked to make jokes that no one else found funny. He was always on the lookout for a scoop, and he lived for digging dirt.

Bonnie rolled her eyes. "He wouldn't..." she muttered.

But he would. He had. Bonnie scooped the trowel out of the compost sack and heard the scrape of metal on metal. She rooted around in the moist black dirt until her fingers closed on a key. She brushed it clean and slid it into the back door's heavy mortice lock. She turned the key.

Clonk.

The door opened. She was in.

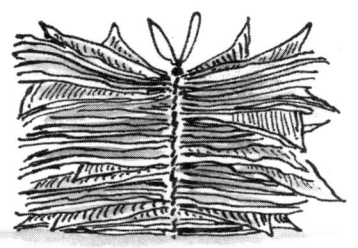

Chapter Eighteen
A Mystery (Unlocked)

Grampa Banks would have to add breaking and entering to the Tab. Although was it *really* breaking and entering if you used a key? Bonnie had not broken anything. Walking through a door was just ... *entering*. That did not sound nearly as bad.

The interior of Maanvi Mallick's home was cluttered. Stacks of magazines and newspapers, bound together with string, leaned against every wall. It looked like he was about to lose the world's biggest game of Tetris.

The hallway was decorated with yellowed newspaper cuttings, old photographs and awards for long-forgotten achievements. Half-empty coffee mugs rested on almost every surface, and wherever there was not a mug, a coffee ring had been left behind.

The focal point of the home was Maanvi Mallick's colossal printing press, right in the middle of his living room. Beside it on the wall was a heavily annotated map of Odde Island, and on a nearby table, Bonnie saw a chunky grey laptop that looked like Mallick had bought it around the time of the Battle of Hastings; the keys were so worn down that none of the letters were visible. Underneath the table, a wastepaper basket was overflowing with crumpled balls of paper.

Whatever else Bonnie might have thought about Maanvi Mallick, she had to admit that the reporter took his job seriously. It would take decades to make sense of the mounds of paperwork that surrounded her. If only Mallick had been more like Iain Percival, he would have had a safe marked *Secret Evidence*, or a folder labelled *Plans (Evil)*.

Bonnie noticed a sloping architect's desk, almost invisible underneath the newspaperman's research. Notes, papers, bills, letters and old editions of the *Odde Argus* were pinned, stuck, glued and occasionally nailed to the desk. A sign at the top of the desk, written in marker pen, read *LOOSE ENDS*.

Bonnie recognized her own face underneath Montgomery Bonbon's moustache. It was a newspaper cutting of *The Widdler* from the time Bonnie had apprehended a piano tuner who was deliberately hiding seafood in her clients' homes and stinking the place out. *PIANO TUNA: Felon is Catch of the Day!* yelled the headline. Maanvi Mallick had circled Montgomery Bonbon's picture and written: *Where is he from??*

The great detective was not alone on the loose ends desk. An IOU addressed to Mr Mallick was clipped to an old photograph of Tobias Waterman. *Owed money all over town* had been jotted next to it in the newspaperman's neat cursive. A telephone bill was pinned up underneath. The last entry for the night of Maude Cragge's death was a one-second telephone call.

That was strange. A one-second call? A second was hardly enough time to say hello, never mind "How's the lighthouse?" It had to be a mistake, surely.

Just as Bonnie began to pull on that loose end of a thought, the sound of footsteps outside the cottage made her ears prick up and she lost her thread. She ducked down and crunched her way into the overflowing mound of crumpled paper under Maanvi Mallick's desk. She did not want to be discovered mid-snoop.

With a *schlup-schlup-schlup*, the footsteps passed from one side of the cottage to the other along the clifftop path. Peeking out, Bonnie recognized the top of Professor Hornville's head bobbing past the window on the way to her cottage next door. Bonnie let herself breathe again, but waited until she was sure she would not be seen crinkling back out of the heap of discarded paper.

"A one-second telephone call," she said to herself, "made to Leerie Lighthouse, from number two-six-four..."

Bonnie thought back to the old-fashioned green telephone she had seen mounted on the wall of the lighthouse. There was only one reason she could think of why a phone call would be so very short.

If a phone was ringing and you did not wish to be distracted...

If a phone was ringing, and you were in the middle of an argument...

If a phone was ringing and *you had murder on your mind* ... might you not pick up the receiver and hang up straight away?

Ring, click, buzzzzz.

The call had been placed at ten at night and—Wait, that could not be right...

Bonnie ran a finger along the bill to be sure. The cheap paper rustled, but the faint grey numbers left her in no doubt. A one-second call had been placed to Leerie Lighthouse at ten o'clock on the night of the storm.

"Oh, what a dolt!" she scolded herself. The telephone number was not a surprise. "Odde Island two-six-four," Roz Baillie had said. It was the number of the Bright Phoebus B & B. The number of Tobias Waterman. What made Bonnie want to kick the wastepaper basket was the *time* of the call.

Tobias Waterman had lied.

The hotelier had told Bonnie that he had spoken with Maude Cragge at eleven on the night of her murder, but that was a lie. There was no record of a call later than ten. In fact, Waterman had called the lighthouse a full hour earlier, and for only one second!

Every suspect's alibi depended on Maude Cragge being alive and well at eleven o'clock. Tobias Waterman had invented a phoney phone call to get someone off the hook. He must have guessed who pushed Maude Cragge.

And that gave *someone* an excellent motive for his murder. Bonnie ripped the phone bill from the desk and folded it into her backpack. She dashed for the back door, eager to share her new clue with Dana and Grampa Banks. She had already taken hold of the door handle when she heard sounds from outside. Ducking down so that she could not be seen through the frosted back door window, she heard something quite unexpected.

Grampa Banks's voice.

"Shall we GO INSIDE your cottage now, MR MALLICK?" he boomed. "To pick up your umbrella, MR MALLICK?"

Bonnie heard a somewhat bewildered reply from Maanvi Mallick, followed by a scuffle of boots approaching the back door. She had not locked the door behind her when she came in. Without thinking, Bonnie found herself sliding the latch to stop Mallick stumbling in on top of her.

Snib.

"Wait, wait, wait!" came Grampa Banks's voice. "Perhaps I could take a quick photo of you before we GO INSIDE? Hmm?"

"Oh, you shutterbugs," said Mallick with a chuckle. "It's all work, work, work with you!"

While the newspaperman posed for a picture, a strange kind of clarity came over Bonnie.

Click, FLASH, grrr...

She knew Grampa Banks was talking in a THEATRICAL VOICE to give her a chance to hide or escape, but that was the last thing on her mind.

She unbolted the door slowly.

Click, FLASH, grrr...

She silently bolted it again.

Click, FLASH, grrr...

In that moment, she knew exactly how Tobias Waterman had been killed.

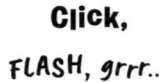

"All right, that's enough snaps," protested Maanvi Mallick. "I don't like the look of those clouds."

Before he had a chance to try the handle, Bonnie unbolted the door and swung it open.

"Who the heck are you?" demanded Mallick, eyes goggling. The reporter looked alarmed by Bonnie's sudden appearance, but he was nowhere near as surprised as Grampa Banks.

"My name's Bonnie; pleased to meet you," said Bonnie, shaking Mallick's hand vigorously. "I'm staying with the Hornvilles next door, and just popped by to borrow a cup of sugar."

"C-cup of ... what?" stammered the newspaperman as Bonnie bowled past him, fizzing with the energy that comes with fresh inspiration.

"The back door was open; hope you don't mind," she explained. "Grampa Banks, great to see you!" Bonnie grabbed her grandfather by both hands. "I need a lift."

"Wait, hold up!" Maanvi Mallick protested, but Bonnie was not going to be derailed. She dragged Grampa Banks towards Bessie, parked near by.

"You should probably lock your back door, Mr Mallick. Lots of dangers about," called Bonnie, bundling Grampa Banks into Bessie's driver's seat. "Don't you read the news?"

Bessie pulled away, and Maanvi Mallick gaped as if he had been spun around ten times blindfolded.

In the passenger seat, Bonnie clenched her fists tightly in her lap. Montgomery Bonbon's timeline had been wrong from the start, and Tobias Waterman's testimony was as flimsy as his toast. The oily hotelier had been covering for Maude Cragge's murderer. He must have imagined that his money troubles were over, now that he knew the killer's secret. But someone had bought his silence with a bonk on the noggin.

When he had burst into Bonnie's room that morning, Tobias Waterman had knocked over Montgomery Bonbon's breakfast bowl of baked beans.

One thing was certain. Tobias Waterman would never spill the beans again.

Day	Time	Area	Number	Direction	Duration	Charges
	14:27	Odde Island	942	Outgoing	00:07:14	0.91
	16:42	Mainland	847 948	Outgoing	00:02:04	0.26
FRI	11:23	Odde Island	294	Outgoing	00:04:14	0.53
	21:59	Odde Island	264	Incoming	00:00:01	0.00

owed money all over town

I.O.U

~~~~~~~~~
mr. Mallick
~~~~~~~~~
~~~ ~~~
~~~~~~

lesueen.

TUNA
ATCH OF

WHERE IS HE FROM??

Chapter Nineteen
The Odde Island Pageant
(a splendid affair, overshadowed very slightly by the murders)

"But Waterman's office door was *locked*, love," said Grampa Banks. "I mean, old man."

He spotted Bonnie retrieving Montgomery Bonbon's moustache from her backpack and fixing it carefully in place.

"I may be getting on a bit, but I know a locked door when I open one," he continued. "I mean, not when I *open* one. But ... when I *see* one."

He thought for a moment.

"I mean, not when I see one..."

While Grampa Banks was losing his way, Bessie

was slowly snaking along a narrow road in the direction of Hillikin Knowe. By now, he had explained, the Odde Island Pageant should have reached the round hill in the middle of the island.

That was, if the costumed villagers had not spent too long frolicking, jingling and mischievously capering about along the way.

"That's precisely the point," said Bonnie, trying to tilt her beret to the correct angle as the ice-cream van sploshed through potholes the size of duck ponds. "A bolted door looks exactly the same as an unbolted door from the outside. And the door really was locked when you tried the handle."

She paused for effect. Up ahead, dark clouds were scowling over Hillikin Knowe.

"Because the killer was still in there."

Grampa Banks's face fell. He looked like he'd just heard that cardigans and loafers were no longer in fashion.

"Come again?"

As the scenery shuffled past the windows, Bonnie attempted to explain the whole locked room puzzle from the start.

"I think Tobias Waterman had worked out who did Maude Cragge in – and why. But, instead of reporting it, he decided to blackmail the murderer."

"Blackmail!" blustered Grampa Banks. "Well, I suppose the guest house could do with new carpets. And walls. And the roof wasn't looking too hot..."

"And according to Maanvi Mallick, Waterman owed money to just about everyone on Odde Island. But the killer, rather than coughing up the cash to keep him quiet, sees an opportunity – and bashes Tobias on the head."

"The fiend!" said Grampa Banks. "Then what?"

"*Alors*," said Bonnie, sliding into Montgomery Bonbon's voice without thinking. "The perpetrator is tidying up the crime scene when you and I enter the guest house. When Bonbon approaches the reception, the killer hides beneath the desk. When we move to the office door, they tiptoe over and crouch on the other side of it ... and this is the part most important..."

Bonnie remembered hiding behind Maanvi Mallick's back door.

"The killer bolts the door."

"So it *was* locked," mumbled Grampa Banks petulantly, before the realization hit him. "You mean the devil was right *there* when I tried the handle?!"

"Mmm-hmm. And when we step outside to summon the constable *espéciale*, the killer seizes another chance. Instead of unbolting the door and escaping straight away, they pull so very hard on the door handle until the little brass bolt, it is torn free. Then they close the door behind them, and simply disappear out of the back entrance."

"So, when young Roz kicked the door in..." Grampa Banks began.

"It was already unlocked," finished Bonnie. "But the broken bolt made us believe it had been locked all along."

"Bloomin' heck," exclaimed Grampa Banks. "Pardon my language, but this killer isn't half good at thinking on their feet! Do you think we'd better tell Inspector Sands?"

"Come on, Baillie lass!" came a distant voice, just audible over the hum of Bessie's engine. "Give it a bit of welly."

It was Inspector Sands, as if summoned by a pageant-day enchantment. Bonnie wound down the passenger window for a better look. Approaching on the road behind them, a crimson-faced Roz Baillie was riding her bicycle. The inspector clung on behind her, one arm wrapped tightly round Roz's waist, and one hand over her eyes.

"Or perhaps," whispered Grampa Banks, eyeing the rear-view mirror thoughtfully, "we should wait until you've worked out who done it? Clue in the inspector later?"

Bonnie nodded as Roz drew parallel with the ice-cream van.

"Maybe", the especial constable wheezed, "a police car ... would have been ... better than a seaplane."

"Well, obviously a car would have been better!" said Inspector Sands. "If I'd known all you had was a flipping two-wheeled doodad, I wouldn't have blown the budget on a flying thingamawotsit. Now pick up the pace: a storm's brewing."

Driving in a former ice-cream van and being overtaken by two police officers who were riding on the same bicycle ought to have been a little embarrassing. But Bonnie's attention was on a fat raindrop plopping onto Bessie's windscreen. With a *crick-crack-crick-crack* more drops followed. Bonnie held her hand out of the passenger window and felt the wind growing stronger.

Rain. Just like the night of the storm, she thought. And then it hit her.

A raindrop – and the answer.

The raindrop landed in the middle of Bonnie's palm. The answer struck somewhere in her unconscious, in the place where detectives poke and prod and chip away at the most troubling mysteries; the place where the inexplicable was made plicable.

Bonnie knew who the murderer was, but there was no time for celebration.

"Bloomin' heck," she said, forgetting to do Montgomery Bonbon's voice. "Step on it, Banks!"

"Ahem... Bessie is actually travelling at her top speed right now," said Grampa Banks sheepishly.

"Well, *keep* stepping on it, then."

"Have you had one of your Eureka Moments, love?"

Bonnie looked out into the gathering storm. "I have. And if I'm right, then Dana's in danger."

Grampa Banks nodded seriously and redoubled his grip on Bessie's steering wheel. Hillikin Knowe rose up ahead of them. With its ring of thorn bushes, it still looked like the top of a monk's head. But this time, pageant-goers were streaming down its slopes. As the weather turned nastier, enormous vegetables rolled, bounced and tumbled downhill. Flaming torches were snuffed out. Jugglers and stilt-walkers competed to see who could look the most ridiculous running for cover.

Bonnie searched the scene for any sign of a giant white onion among the thorn bushes.

Bessie *thrududududududed* over a cattle grid, where Roz Baillie appeared to have parted company with her bicycle. The especial constable was hanging upside down by the side of the road, the seat of her trousers tangled in a chicken wire fence. As they rumbled past, Inspector Sands, miraculously unharmed, was busy berating her.

"Come on, come on," said Bonnie, willing the ice-cream van to move faster. She still could see no sign of Dana.

They approached the oblong-shaped patch of rough ground which passed for the Hillikin Knowe car park. A number of holidaymakers, laughing and singing in spite of the rain, were rambling down towards their cars and the shelter of Odde Harbour. Or perhaps, thought Bonnie, towards the smugglers' hideout. She had spotted Reuben Ribble with a great big leek costume under his arm, tramping down a bank.

"*Excusez-me!*" she called out of the window as they swung into the car park. "*Excusez-ME!*"

"Is that you, Mr Detective?" sang out Reuben Ribble, his red face cheerier than usual. "How d'you get out of costume so fast?"

"The onion, Monsieur, where is the onion?"

Reuben Ribble loped over towards Bessie and leaned into the driver's window, a wry twinkle in his eye. "Now why would I know anything about onions?"

"Monsieur Ribble," snapped Bonnie, her moustache radiating authority, "unless you wish for *everyone* to know your onions, you will listen most carefully, and do precisely as Montgomery Bonbon instructs. Understand?"

Reuben Ribble scratched his stubbly chin and nodded solemnly, clearly realizing that the fun was over.

"First, tell to me: where is the person in the onion costume?"

"I don't rightly know," said Ribble. "Went off ahead with Miss Bunch. Down the hill towards Solan

Cliffs, I reckon. We were meant to follow, but it started to rain so we're calling it a day."

"Solan Cliffs..." echoed Bonnie, and she felt her spirits sagging. She knew what needed to be done, and there was no time to waste.

"Second, Monsieur Ribble," she continued, "give to me the key to Leerie Lighthouse."

"Now, hang on," said the assistant keeper, checking his watch, "I'm supposed to wind up the mechanism soon."

"Come on, man!" cried Grampa Banks. "D'you think this is a time for games? Hand it over!"

Few people had heard Grampa Banks speak like that. Bonnie quickly found the lighthouse key in her possession.

"And finally, Monsieur Ribble, this is most important." Bonnie leaned over and made sure she had the soggy smuggler's attention. "Follow this road a short distance until you come upon Inspecteur Sands of the Widdling Constabulary."

A sudden clap of thunder drowned out whatever it was Reuben Ribble had to say about the Widdlington Constabulary.

"Find the inspecteur, and tell to her to go to Leerie Lighthouse – post-haste!"

"Post-haste!" repeated Grampa Banks emphatically.

"Post-haste." Ribble nodded obediently.

"There Inspecteur Sands will meet Montgomery Bonbon ... and arrest Miss Bunch for murder."

Chapter Twenty
The Storm

Thunderstorms live for drama. It is a plain meteorological fact that a thunderstorm will always turn up when things are about to kick off. The instant a forbidden tomb is cracked open, the moment an ancient family curse is fulfilled, the very second a detective enters into a clifftop chase with a murderous schoolteacher – in rolls a thunderstorm.

"There they are!" cried Grampa Banks, as a splash of lightning lit up the grey sky like the flash from his old camera. Bonnie saw Miss Bunch and Dana silhouetted against the low clouds.

Miss Bunch was wearing her flowery hat; Dana was encased in the onion costume that had been meant for Montgomery Bonbon. The strange-looking pair had left the crowds behind and were picking their way across the rain-slick cliffs on the approach to Leerie Lighthouse.

"She thinks I'm in there," murmured Bonnie, as much to herself as to Grampa Banks. "Pull in!"

They had gone as far as Bessie could take them. The rocks of Solan Cliffs rose up ahead in great crooked columns, like stacks of dishes left there by a prehistoric giant who simply would not help out in the kitchen.

"You there!" called Grampa Banks, clambering out of the ice-cream van. "Stop!"

"Halt! *Arrêtez! Achtung!*" yelled Bonnie, already in front of him, but the wind carried their voices out to sea.

Dana was striding ahead of Miss Bunch along a narrow track. Sure-footed and as confident as ever, Bonnie's friend must have believed the pageant was still going on around her. From inside that stupid costume, could Dana even see how close she was to plunging over the sheer cliff?

Bonnie cursed herself for not putting the pieces

together sooner. Miss Bunch must have thought Montgomery Bonbon was onto her when they questioned her last night. Clearly she had planned for the onion to take a tumble during the frenzy of the pageant, under the guise of stamping out the forbidden fruit (or verboten vegetable). She had not counted on the storm driving everyone home, but it was obvious that Miss Bunch was not going to let a bit of rain get in the way of another *accident*.

Miss Bunch was better at thinking on her feet than she was at travelling on them. The schoolteacher tiptoed uncertainly over loose stones, her arms outstretched like an amateur acrobat. Now and again, she managed to give the onion costume a little shove, bringing Dana closer and closer and closer to the edge.

Bonnie could not afford to waste another second.

She clambered over wet rocks and squeezed through fissures. Rain was running down her coat; her hair and moustache were drenched, but she pressed on. She hauled herself up, and planted herself at the highest point she could reach. She called out, across a wide ravine.

"Dana! Fräulein Bunch!"

It was no use. Bonnie was too far away. The wind, the rain and the roar of the sea all conspired to silence her. Below her, Grampa Banks was fighting against the storm, plodding determinedly through a maze of intersecting footpaths, towards Dana and Miss Bunch. He showed no regard for what the weather was doing to his favourite cardigan. But he was not going to reach them in time either.

It was the thunderstorm itself, with its love of the dramatic, which came to Bonnie's aid. A sheet of lightning turned the sky brilliant white just as Miss Bunch twisted her ankle, and the wind almost carried her flowery hat off into oblivion.

As the schoolteacher recovered her hat, she caught sight of Montgomery Bonbon. She gaped for a moment, looking back and forth between the giant onion and the great detective.

At last, realizing that she had been tricked, she pointed a finger and shrieked.

"Monsieuuuur!"

Bonnie did not need to be able to hear Miss Bunch

to recognize the word. The schoolteacher carelessly shoved Dana aside, hitched up her dress and headed for the real Montgomery Bonbon.

Dana wobbled, and stumbled and slid and rolled...

Bonnie's heart was in her mouth as she watched, powerless. Miss Bunch was hobbling and clambering towards Bonnie, with her weight on her good ankle and an expression of trembling fury. And in the same instant, Dana was rolling along the pitted clifftop path, legs wriggling as if the onion bulb were trying to take root. One of her hands burst out of the sodden papier mâché and flailed helplessly. A green shoot, reaching for the sun.

There was nothing Bonnie could do to help her friend as Dana tumbled towards the precipice. The deductive genius of Montgomery Bonbon was no use out here. Dana needed the honed reflexes of a former ice-cream vendor.

As Dana rolled on towards the brink, another hand reached out. This hand was firm, dependable and exceptionally well manicured. It grasped Dana's hand, stopping her just inches away from the precipitous drop.

The hand belonged to Grampa Banks. His cardigan was soaked. His cravat was askew. His crêpe-soled shoes looked like total crêpe. But in Montgomery Bonbon's eyes, Grampa Banks had never looked like a better assistant. Bonnie longed to see both him and Dana safe and dry, but she could not dilly-dally. Miss Bunch was closing in on Montgomery Bonbon.

Bonnie scrambled down a slope and splashed her way along a track that was fast turning into a stream. Rainwater rushed down the rocks on either side, bubbled over her feet and drowned her shoes.

Was there a chance that Inspector Sands had got her message? Could the inspector already be making her way through the labyrinth of intersecting paths that spiralled up, up, up towards Leerie Lighthouse? Bonnie had to believe that Reuben Ribble had been trustworthy enough to pass on her instructions, and that Inspector Sands had been smart enough to do as she was told.

It was a real long shot.

Bonnie had no choice. She had to head towards the lighthouse. It was her only hope of handing the killer over to Inspector Sands. And as long as the water was flowing downhill towards her, Bonnie knew she was moving in the right direction.

She ran, occasionally glancing over her shoulder to make sure that Miss Bunch was still limping after her. Now and again, she caught sight of Grampa Banks carefully rolling Dana away from the cliff edge.

Every time Bonnie came to a dead end, she expected to feel the schoolteacher's hands grasping at her. But eventually she saw the familiar red stripe of Leerie Lighthouse up ahead. She knew then how seasick, storm-tossed sailors must have felt when a winking lantern told them two things: firstly, that they had found land; and secondly, that new dangers lay ahead.

There was no one waiting for Montgomery Bonbon when Bonnie reached the lighthouse. It was too much to expect Widdlington Constabulary to handle a dramatic finale on their own. She hurried towards the lighthouse door, fumbling with Reuben Ribble's key. Behind her, she could almost hear the sound of Miss Bunch's uneven steps in the slurry of gravel and mud that surrounded the lighthouse.

Click.

The whitewashed door swung open. Bonnie hurried inside and closed the door behind her. It would be easy enough to lock it again, but that would give Miss Bunch a chance to escape. And it would leave Grampa Banks and Dana stuck outside with a killer.

No. Bonnie needed to find a way to trap Miss Bunch, and she had mere seconds before the schoolteacher came bursting through the lighthouse door. She ran. Past the golden fleece which was really more of a parka, past Maude Cragge's photographs and past her fishy drawings.

Spurred on by adrenaline, Bonnie pelted up the spiral stairs, taking the steps two at a time. It felt like she was running on someone else's legs, and whoever that person was, they were going to need a good long rest tomorrow. And breakfast in bed too. A glance at the mechanism in the middle of the lighthouse told Bonnie that Reuben Ribble had spoken the truth. The clockwork mechanism had been wound up before he left for the pageant. Now it was ticking down, down, down towards its end.

That gave Bonnie an idea.

Whoosh!

The door burst open, and Miss Bunch blew in on a gust of wind that whistled the whole height of the lighthouse. Her hair was wild, her clothes torn.

"*Monsieueueueur?*" she called in her sing-song voice as she mounted the stairs. "Oh, Monsieur? I think there's been a mistake!"

"*Ja*," called Bonnie, sidling up the steps, "there have been two most *deadly* mistakes, Fräulein. You murdered Maude Cragge and Tobias Waterman. *J'accuse!*"

"But those were accidents, Monsieur," protested Miss Bunch, squelching up the steps behind Bonnie. "You can't really believe I go around killing people!"

"I believe," sniffed Bonnie, climbing further up the staircase, "that your crimes were committed on the spur of the moment. I give to you the top marks for improvisation, Fräulein Bunch. But murder ... is being murder."

"I'm sure I don't know what you mean," said Miss Bunch, laughing a false laugh as she continued to climb.

Bonnie was nearing the top of the spiral stairs. She took a chance and peered down over the balustrade. Her head swam, and the scene below her seemed to stretch and swirl. Montgomery Bonbon was not good with heights. She could hear Miss Bunch splapping closer and caught glimpses of her ragged outfit through gaps in the floorboards.

Maude Cragge must have found herself in just this situation, thought Bonnie, but without the advantage of knowing how dangerous Miss Bunch could be. Above her head, there was nothing but the iron hatch to the lighthouse's viewing deck. The very top of the lighthouse was an excellent place to fall from – and not a very good place to hide.

The splaps came faster and faster, spiralling towards Bonnie. Any moment now, Miss Bunch would be in sight. Bonnie could not wait for Grampa Banks or Inspector Sands to turn up and save the day. Besides, that was hardly Montgomery Bonbon's style.

It was foolish even to consider venturing out onto the viewing deck in a storm. It was dangerous. It was almost certain not to work. But if she wanted to bring the killer to justice, Bonnie needed time to outfox Miss Bunch. She needed to catch her opponent off balance. Bonnie had to beat Miss Bunch at her own game and *improvise*.

It took all Bonnie's strength to lever the hatch open.

"Stop right there!" commanded Miss Bunch from somewhere just below.

Bonnie pulled herself up. Up and out, onto the narrow wooden walkway encircling the lighthouse lantern. The storm winds stung her cheeks and tried to peel off her moustache. The boards beneath her feet were wet. The sweep of the lighthouse lantern was dazzling.

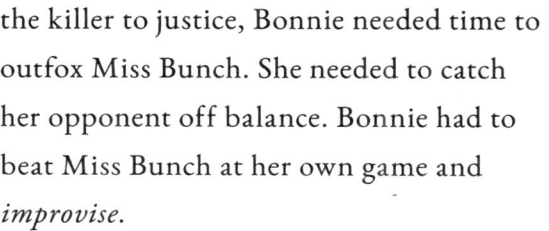

wwWWOOoouuum

Bonnie squeezed her eyes shut. She groped for the metal handrail that ran around the deck's outer rim. It felt like ice to the touch, and a lot less sturdy than it had looked from the ground. She inched her way gingerly around the viewing deck.

wwWWOOouuum

The lantern turned again, and Bonnie saw Miss Bunch emerge from the hatch – bedraggled, billowing, splashing her palms down on the boards and heaving herself up.

"Well now, Monsieur," she called out over the cacophony of the storm. "Hands up if you know the answer, because I have a little question *pour vous*."

Miss Bunch cupped her face in her hands and smiled a counterfeit smile. All the anger Bonnie had seen on the clifftop was hidden behind it. The schoolteacher looked like she was going to hand out lemon sherbets for the right answer.

"What makes you think it was me?"

IMPORTANT

- cupola
- Lantern
- Hatch
- ladder
- windows
- viewing Deck/gallery
- Quarters
- Galley/kitchen
- Cragge's workshop + office
- Needlessly complex winding mechanism
- Entrance

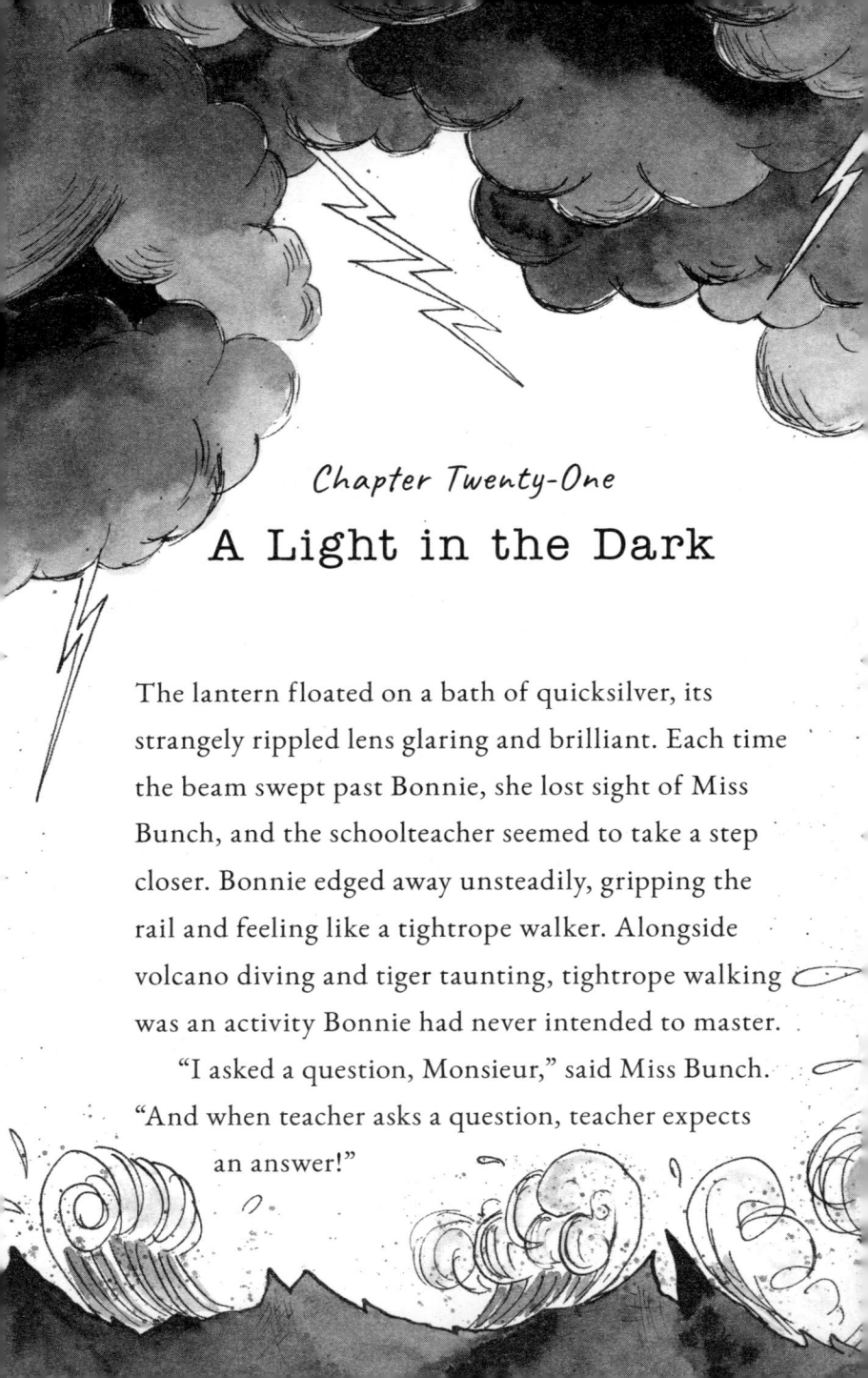

Chapter Twenty-One
A Light in the Dark

The lantern floated on a bath of quicksilver, its strangely rippled lens glaring and brilliant. Each time the beam swept past Bonnie, she lost sight of Miss Bunch, and the schoolteacher seemed to take a step closer. Bonnie edged away unsteadily, gripping the rail and feeling like a tightrope walker. Alongside volcano diving and tiger taunting, tightrope walking was an activity Bonnie had never intended to master.

"I asked a question, Monsieur," said Miss Bunch. "And when teacher asks a question, teacher expects an answer!"

Bonnie longed to look down to see if Grampa Banks or Inspector Sands had reached the lighthouse. But she did not trust herself to glance over the railing. The whole building felt like it was swaying nauseatingly in the wind, and Bonnie did not dare take her eyes off Miss Bunch.

"Come now, what makes you think I could hurt anyone?" said Miss Bunch, putting on a deeply wounded expression.

"It was the rain," Bonnie called back. "The rain, it betrays you, Fräulein."

Miss Bunch stuck out her tongue, as if someone had offered her a gravy flavoured lollipop.

"The rain?"

"*Ja!* Maude Cragge, she was not wearing the golden fleece when she died. This tells to Bonbon that the lighthouse keeper was pushed *before* the storm began."

As the lantern turned again, Miss Bunch took another lopsided step forward.

"And what's that got to do—"

wwWWOOouuum

"—with me?" asked Miss Bunch, eyes wide like a wet puppy.

Bonnie felt her way along the railing, keeping her distance. She could hardly tell the pounding of her heart from the *tick-tock* of the clockwork lighthouse.

"You lied to Bonbon about seeing the Lady Wallop out and – how do you say? – about."

"That's not a lie," said Miss Bunch. "I did see her."

"*Oui*, but you did not see her *during* the storm. The Lady Wallop tells to Bonbon that she completed her journey that night *before* the rain started to fall."

"So what?"

"And so, Fräulein, during the time you claimed to be at home, you must have been most distant from the schoolhouse. Or else you could not have seen Lady Wallop driving from the Peeble Beach to the old Martello tower."

Miss Bunch stared blankly, a blobule of rain dongling from the tip of her nose.

"Her word against mine," she said dismissively, with one of her fluttering hand gestures.

"The guest house," Bonnie pressed on, "it is opposite your home. The always nosey Tobias Waterman, he sees Fräulein Bunch sneaking back after killing Maude Cragge, before the lighthouse stops? Is that not so?"

Bonnie was trying to freeze Miss Bunch in place with a stare, but it was not working. Her moustache was too wet and drooping to do the job. The schoolteacher kept shuffling closer. Bonnie could almost feel her straggly hair. She shrank back, and went on.

"Tobias Waterman, he tries to blackmail Fräulein Bunch. But Fräulein Bunch decides ... *non*. She cannot trust her secret with a man who has the tongue so loose. She loses her temper, and Tobias has the little accident in the office room."

"Nobody saw me," said Miss Bunch, producing a silk handkerchief from her frilly sleeve. "I mean, nobody saw *anything*."

wwwWWWOOoouuum

Bonnie watched in horror as Miss Bunch blew her nose on Tobias Waterman's red handkerchief. That snot rag was *evidence*, and one of the main things you are not supposed to do with a piece of evidence is blow your nose on it. With a cheeky wink, Miss Bunch held the piece of silk over the railing. It flapped wetly in the wind ... and vanished into the night.

Bonnie could feel the case against Miss Bunch crumbling beneath her feet.

Then came a voice from the still-open hatch. A voice that made a very soggy detective feel warm inside.

"Bonbon? Bonbon old man?"

It was Grampa Banks, somewhere below them in the lighthouse. Miss Bunch hissed and retreated to the hatch. She threw it closed with a resounding *clang* and dragged a waterlogged toolbox on top of it.

"Give yourself up, Fräulein," said Bonnie, hoping that Montgomery Bonbon sounded more confident than she felt. "You have no other way down!"

Miss Bunch smiled a very strange smile.

"There is one other way down," she said. "Just ask Maude Cragge."

Bam!

The toolbox jumped as Grampa Banks hammered on the other side of the hatch.

"Widdlington Police!" came another voice. Inspector Sands. "What's your game, Bonbon? Dragging us all the way out to a bloomin' thingumabob?"

"The monsieur and I are just having a very friendly chat!" Miss Bunch called back in her clearest teacher's voice. She held the hatch closed with her good foot. "The hatch seems to have jammed."

Bam! Bam!

For a second, the iron hatch opened, just a crack, and Bonnie caught a glimpse of her grandfather's worried face. Squeezed in next to him was

Dana (deathly frightened), along with Inspector Sands (completely baffled). Miss Bunch redoubled her efforts and the hatch door slammed closed again.

"Now listen carefully," Miss Bunch said, speaking through gritted teeth, "because I wouldn't want to lose my temper again, Monsieur. I am going to open this hatch, and then you are going to explain that this was all a terrible misunderstanding, *tu comprends*?"

She had seemed like a harmless eccentric in the cellar of the schoolhouse, surrounded by her prized vegetables. Bonnie remembered thinking that there was nothing fishy about Miss Bunch's costumes. Her internal fishy-o-meter had let her down.

The dazzling beam swept around again.

wwWWOOouuum

Inspiration, like a clap of thunder, like Grampa Banks's camera, like the revolving lantern of a clockwork lighthouse, often comes with a flash.

There was nothing fishy about those costumes. But the costume designs Bonnie had seen right here in the lighthouse, with their oversized fish heads and scaly tails, they were fishier than a dollop of trout ice cream. And those designs were labelled MC.

BAM, BAM, BAM!

"Well, Monsieur," said Miss Bunch, fraying at the edges, "do we understand each other?"

Bonnie tried to steady her breathing. At last she had spotted an opportunity to catch Miss Bunch off balance.

"First," she said, "one more question. Do you not think, Fräulein Bunch, that your costume designs are a little ... silly, *non*?"

Miss Bunch's expression froze. "You know very well that my designs are a triumph. You said as much yourself, Monsieur."

Bonnie shook her head, creating a little moustache rainstorm.

"Oh, I see," Miss Bunch snarled. "You're trying to provoke me. Trying to distract teacher, are we? It won't work. The whole island loves my costumes."

"Not the whole island, Fräulein," said Bonnie, with one eyebrow raised. "Bonbon, he prefers the designs more tasteful. More sophisticated. More *je ne sais quoi*. The designs of..."

Bonnie pretended to think for a moment.

"Maude Cragge, *par exemple*?"

Miss Bunch reacted as if Bonnie had flopped a wet haddock into her cornflakes. Her face contorted in shock and disgust.

"Don't be revolting, Monsieur!" she said. "My designs have ten times as much je ne sais quoi as her rotten, amateurish, ugly, stinking—"

"I think, perhaps," interrupted Bonnie, "that you did not plan to kill her?"

"Of course I didn't plan it! I just came here to talk, but she made me so cross. She wouldn't listen. She just kept working. Winding this; mending that.

She didn't understand!"

wwwwwWWWOOOOOOoooouuumm

The lantern seemed to be rotating more slowly. If Bonnie was right, the clockwork mechanism was winding down. That meant the moment she had been waiting for was approaching.

"Not like you, Monsieur, ever so clever. Always asking your needling little questions."

She took a step towards Bonnie. "You understand that a Bunch..."

Step.

"...has *always* designed the costumes..."

Step.

"...for the Odde Island Pageant."

Step.

"It is..."

Step.

"TRADITION!"

Her last word came out as a roar. Almost everyone Bonnie had met on Odde Island had told her how seriously they took tradition here. For Miss Bunch, it was *deadly* serious. The schoolteacher launched herself towards Bonnie.

Blooorororororong!

The great gong sound from deep in the lighthouse's clockwork heart reverberated throughout the building. Bonnie held on to the handrail as the sound shook the tower and rattled the glass panes of the lantern. In one stroke, Miss Bunch was staggering, stumbling, grasping for a handhold.

Thank goodness that the people who built clockwork lighthouses thought keepers were too thick to remember to wind them up, thought Bonnie.

wwwwwWWWOO—

The lantern began what might have been its final sweep. When the beam was on Bonnie, she could not see Miss Bunch. That meant that when the beam was on Miss Bunch, Miss Bunch could not see Bonnie.

Bonnie was glad she did not have to say that ten times, fast.

When the lantern turned its glare on Miss Bunch, Bonnie let go of the handrail and began to run away from the light, around the viewing deck, towards the hatch.

BAM,

BAM,

BAM!

Without Miss Bunch to help hold down the hatch, the toolbox leaped into the air.

"Stop!" shrieked Miss Bunch, clinging on to the railing. "The bell does not dismiss you; I dismiss you!"

Her stern schoolteacher's voice had no effect on Montgomery Bonbon. He was, after all, a gentleman detective and not a ten-year-old girl.

Bonnie ran towards the hatch, and into the arms of Grampa Banks.

Bonnie's eyes were closed. Her face was buried in a rain-soaked cardigan that would soon be on its way to be dry cleaned. She did not see Inspector Sands clambering inelegantly onto the viewing deck. She only heard the words: "Miss Pneumonia Bunch, I am placing you under arrest."

Epilogue

Bonnie stepped out of the lighthouse. She breathed in the rich, earthy smells of a retreating storm. The rain had become no more than drizzle. Clouds were beginning to lift. The thunder and lightning had gone away, in search of a mad scientist making a Frankenstein.

A watercolour sun shone down on Leerie Lighthouse. When she got back to Widdlington, Bonnie thought, she was going to write such a bad review for Odde Island as a holiday destination.

Grampa Banks had helped Bonnie down the lighthouse stairs. Now he was gently pressing her crooked moustache back into place. Next he was wringing Odde Island rainwater out of her beret.

"Well done, love," he said, before catching himself. "I mean, bloomin' good work, old bean. Excuse my language."

Dana Hornville had recovered her cool demeanour and was leaning nonchalantly against the wall of the lighthouse. Her look was spoiled only slightly by the remnants of the onion outfit around her waist. Miss Bunch's masterpiece had been reduced to a splayed skeleton by the storm. Bonnie wanted to run over and give Dana a hug – onion and all – but she restrained herself.

She extended a hand stiffly. "*Merci*, Fräulein Hornville," she said, barely holding back a grin. "You were most helpful and most courageous."

"Delighted to be of assistance, Monsieur," replied Dana, pretending to curtsey.

She draped her hand into Bonnie's, like a princess, and they both started to giggle. Bonnie was relieved to

hear Dana's voice, but *monsieur* was a word she had heard enough for one holiday.

She let go of Dana's hand as the *clomp, clomp, clomp* of Inspector Sands's boots grew louder.

The inspector locked the lighthouse, with Miss Bunch still protesting her innocence inside. As she rattled and banged at the whitewashed door, Bonnie reflected that this was one locked room the schoolteacher was not going to escape from.

Widdlington's finest did not look thrilled about having been caught in the storm.

"Why'd you have to chase her all the way out here?" asked Inspector Sands, frowning up at the lighthouse as if it had been built on an inaccessible outcrop specifically to annoy her. "I don't fancy walking all the way back with a double murderer."

"Perhaps the station will send a helicopter to pick you up?" suggested Dana.

For a second, Inspector Sands's face was brighter than the lantern of Leerie Lighthouse.

"Too right they will!" she said, rubbing her hands together. "I wonder how big it will be? You know, it was touch and go for a while, but I'm glad I finally solved the case."

Grampa Banks's hand on Bonnie's shoulder warned her not to say anything rash.

"Congratulations, Inspecteur," Bonnie said finally.

"It is only a shame that Bonbon could not recover Tobias Waterman's red handkerchief. It proved that Miss Bunch was at the scene of the crime when he died."

"I might be able to help there..." came the strangely muffled voice of Roz Baillie.

The especial constable emerged from behind a rocky edifice, dragging her mangled police bike behind her.

"Blimey, Roz lass!" said Inspector Sands. "What on earth have you got on your mug?"

Roz Baillie's face, usually pink and enthusiastic, was completely hidden behind Tobias Waterman's wet red handkerchief.

"It landed on me about quarter of an hour ago," she mumbled. "I didn't want to touch it, in case it were evidence."

Grampa Banks clapped his hands, and Inspector Sands levitated with delight.

"Nice one, Roz Baillie, you beauty!" said Inspector Sands. "Oi, Bonbon, Mr Thingy, little Dana Wotsit – where are you off to now?"

Bonnie had already begun the long, weary walk back to Bessie. She paused.

"I think, Inspecteur, that Montgomery Bonbon should like to take" – she smiled at Dana and Grampa Banks – "the little holiday."

"Hold up a minute! Before you and your little sidekicks toddle off," said Inspector Sands, lowering her voice to something approximating a whisper, "how exactly did I solve the case?"

You may care to know that, in the end, Roz Baillie was elected Grand Maven of the Order of the Golden Fleece, to the surprise of almost everybody – especially Roz Baillie.

Even more unexpectedly, it was Iain Percival who proposed an Onion Amnesty on the first Wednesday of each month. It seemed that something had happened to the exciseman in the run-up to the Odde Island Pageant which had changed him for the better.

It was even rumoured that he enjoyed an onion himself, now and again. But on that subject, Lady Wallop refused to comment.

Leerie Lighthouse was left in the charge of Reuben

Ribble, who continued his nightly activities that were none of your business. In fact, he had no idea what you were talking about. Maanvi Mallick turned his journalistic career around. He ghostwrote Inspector Sands's book, *The Odde Island Murders: An Inspector Sands Mystery*. Which was all very well, but Bonnie could not understand why bookshops kept shelving it in the non-fiction section.

Professor Rita Hornville abandoned her research into the folk practices of Odde Island in favour of studying a less dangerous subject. The last Bonnie heard, she was looking into bear-wrestling in the Ural Mountains.

Dana Hornville became the treasurer (and founder member) of the Official Montgomery Bonbon Admirers' Society. As for Bonnie Montgomery, the ten-year-old girl from Widdlington, she looked forward to nothing more than lounging around, drinking mint tea and eating toast.

Proper toast, as well. Not the kind you can see through if you hold it up to the light.

Before she returned to Widdlington, Bonnie spent

one whole day on the Odde Island sands with Grampa Banks and Dana Hornville: an entire day without murder. During which one sandcastle was built, one piece of fossilized coral was found, and one Grampa Banks was buried up to his neck.

When they got home, Bonnie's mum could not understand how a nice older gentleman could ruin so many cardigans in a single trip.

AUTHOR'S NOTE

Thank you for finishing Montgomery Bonbon's second book!

That is, unless you're reading this bit in a bookshop or library. If that's the case, you must take this book to the counter immediately and shout/whisper, "I have exceptionally good taste and would like to purchase/borrow Montgomery Bonbon's latest, thrilling whodunit!"

Then read the whole book until you get back to this point...

Keep reading...

Did you solve the case? If so, well done! If not, don't worry – I'm sure you'll solve the next one. Thank you for spending your time with Bonnie Montgomery. And thanks to my editor, Gráinne, for helping me with the long words.

Alasdair Beckett-King
Ivory Towers, 2023

Alasdair Beckett-King is a multi-award-winning comedian and writer. He has taken critically lauded stand-up shows to the Edinburgh Festival Fringe, performed comedy on BBC radio and television panel shows, co-written an award-winning video game and his viral internet sketches have amused and annoyed people across the globe. Alasdair's first book, *Montgomery Bonbon: Murder at the Museum*, was selected as the Indie Book of the Month by independent booksellers across the UK.

Claire Powell is a bestselling children's book illustrator who began making books in 2016 and has never looked back. Her collaborations with Kes Gray, Simon Farnaby and Beth Lincoln have all topped the children's book charts.

MONTGOMERY BONBON'S

next case

COMING SOON